Angry House

By

ALEXIS KENNEDY

ISBN: 978-1-946212-28-3
Title Wave Publishing, LLC
Union, MO
https://authoralexiskennedy.com
Cover design by Xcite! DesignZ
EAL Editing Services

"When you write, you escape into another world and another you that you once knew nothing about." —Alexis Kennedy

Books by Alexis Kennedy

Bound Through Blood

Under the Blood Moon (Hearts on Fire Book 1)

Two Faced

Scandalous

Angry House

Birthright (Destiny Bound Book 1)

Indelible (Two Faced book 2)

Gods and Angels

Lycan Moon (Hearts on Fire Book 2)

Deadly Games (Elusive Killers Book 1)

Karma-Summon the Serpent (Destiny Bound Book 2)

PROLOGUE

Brooklyn, NY

Rhett Shaw stared at the blinking cursor on the blank screen while Mötley Crüe blared through the stereo in the background. He ran his calloused hands over his tired eyes and leaned back, forcing the chair to make an awful creaking sound. This had become a habit lately, and his editor wasn't any happier about it than he was. He was a slave to his emotions—a prisoner to his broken heart—keeping his thoughts preoccupied with the past instead of with the book in front of him.

Grumbling a slew of swear words, he pulled himself to his feet and crossed the room to look out the window at the crowded city streets of Brooklyn below. He was tired of that sight, of those sounds, and of the smell of Chinese food mixed with curry—he was tired of the life he had here. He no longer had ties to the city.

His wife, Laura, had unexpectedly passed away almost three years ago, leaving him with a shattered heart. Friends had tried to console him, but he withdrew from the world and fell into a black abyss, quitting his full-time job as a carpenter to become the reclusive writer he is now.

He'd been working on his first book when she died, and she'd always been such an inspiration to him that he felt compelled to finish it no matter what—he owed it to her. Therefore, he burned the midnight oil until it was completed a few months later.

To his surprise, *Wolfsbane* had been an immediate success, as had its sequel, *Wolfsbane— The Blood of Dragons*. Currently, they were still performing much better in sales than he'd ever expected.

Rhett's editor, Dave Sage, was relentlessly pressuring him for another hit, but he had nothing to offer, and he was tired of admitting it.

Nearly every time he typed out a new paragraph, he ended up changing his mind and erasing it—ideas weren't sticking as if his computer screen was made of Teflon. He supposed this was the norm, and he'd just gotten lucky on his first two books.

Part of the problem was he was trying his hand at crime fiction this time—he wanted a break from the paranormal romance genre. He didn't think he could write any more romance when his heart was still breaking. Every thought of Laura made his throat close and his empty chest tighten.

The somber thirty-two-year-old stared out the window at the happy people dashing up and down the streets and felt restless. He wanted to feel happiness again. He wanted to write again. He *needed* to make some major changes in his life.

Rhett's gray eyes scanned his ugly fifth-floor apartment. He despised the yellowed walls bleeding mouse-chewed insulation and the rusty wall vents that were furry with dust.

"I'm done here," he announced to the grimy room with a firm nod.

In the hall closet, there was still an orderly stack of moving boxes from when he'd moved into the hovel a month ago. He'd kept them because he wanted to try the place out first. However, no place felt like home without Laura, and that just made it even easier to pack up and leave.

CHAPTER ONE

Pulling away from the curb, Rhett waved goodbye to his friend Jeremy, who had decided to sublease the shabby apartment on behalf of his younger brother.

"It's his first apartment, so it doesn't need to be much," Jeremy had assured him after seeing the place.

Rhett left the apartment fully furnished for the younger man, except for a small writing desk that was now stuffed inside the back of his 2010 Jeep Grand Cherokee. Most of his dishes and linens remained behind as well.

Laura had been the cook, so he got used to surviving mostly on beans and weenies, frozen TV dinners, and soup with crackers. He probably would've wasted away by now if it weren't for the calories from the added assortment of packaged junk food and occasional takeout.

Nine stoplights later, Rhett looked into the rearview mirror and mentally waved goodbye to Brooklyn. He was on I-91 N and would cross the Vermont border in about six hours. He had no destination in mind—he figured he'd know the place when he saw it—but a map lay neatly folded next to him in the passenger seat just in case he got lost.

Then again, maybe that's what I need—to just get lost somewhere where no one knows me.

It's not as if he was leaving anyone behind. Jeremy was the only person he kept in touch with from his previous life.

His face fell as he thought about how disappointed in him Laura would be. She would be heartbroken to see that he'd lost so many friends all because of her death. Rhett's friends had tried to be there for him while he grieved, but his all-consuming sadness pushed them away.

That's when writing became important to him. According to a therapist, whom he only saw once, it was probably because that was his way to escape the pain of reality. Now, though, since he couldn't concentrate on writing, he just felt used and dried-up—exhausted.

He was still reflecting hours later as he slowly drove past the houses dotting the small town of Winhall, Vermont.

As he admired the picturesque homes with children playing on their manicured lawns, he dug deep to find a glimmer of hope—a piece of the former life he had when things had felt like some semblance of "normal."

Fighting back tears, he made a silent promise to himself to change his ways. Undeniably, he'd have to start slowly, so finding a place in the middle of town was not ideal for him. For now, he needed to avoid the noise—the crowds—so he just kept on driving.

He needed to find a place in the country to rent or buy, hoping that the newfound privacy and quiet setting would inspire him. Of course, that wouldn't help him reconnect to society, but he could always work on that part later—he needed to get his book done first.

For the first time in a long while, Rhett saw himself smiling in the review mirror. His decision already made him feel better.

GET
OUT

Rhett's stomach rumbled to remind him that he hadn't eaten anything all day, so he pulled into the McDonald's Drive-Thru for a hamburger.

Noticing his New York license plates and packed Jeep, the cashier told him, "Welcome to Winhall," as she handed him his food.

"Thank you," he mumbled and pulled forward into a vacant spot to eat his burger.

After his quick lunch, he stopped off at the Shell station to fill up and buy a local street map.

Once he reached the outskirts of town, he kept his eyes peeled for realty signs and soon discovered a couple of places to mark on his map. One location was having an open house, so he dropped off to have a look.

"Hello there. I'm Tom Kidd, the seller's realtor," said a portly man with silver hair edging his otherwise balding scalp, and he extended a thick meaty hand to Rhett.

Rhett looked down at the hand before taking it. "Hello. I was driving by and saw the house," he replied with a sense of uneasiness.

Mr. Kidd looked at the packed Jeep and gave a small nod in its direction. "It looks like you are all ready to move in," he observed.

Rhett's gaze followed his and then dropped down to his shoes. "Well, I'm trying to find a place."

"I notice an accent. Where are you from? New York, right?"

"Yes, I'm moving from Brooklyn," Rhett confirmed.

"So, you're a city boy, huh? What are you doing out in the sticks then?" Mr. Kidd prodded.

There was no way Rhett was going to tell the man his life story—he was not that kind of person—so, he instead just replied with, "I'm looking for a change." It was true after all.

The realtor chuckled, "I'm sure it'll be quite the change for you. We aren't fast-paced around these parts like you New Yorkers are."

Now it was Rhett's turn to chuckle. Nothing about him was fast-paced these days; in fact, he'd probably fit right in with the locals. He looked around the yard at the shrubs and flowers as well as the foundation of the two-story brick house. It was bigger than he needed, and a tear stung his eyes as he could hear voices inside his head telling him, "You are young. You could remarry and have a family someday." But he knew he wouldn't. No one would ever replace the empty hole in his heart left by Laura. No one could complete that part of his life again.

"So, like I was saying, the house is ready to move in, and the owners have left wiggle room on the price," Mr. Kidd said, interrupting his thoughts. He'd been talking the entire time, but Rhett had briefly tuned him out.

"Umm," Rhett mumbled and looked up at the house while running a hand over his stubble-covered chin. "I'm sorry, but it's just too damn big." Then, without further explanation, he spun on his heel and jogged to the Jeep with more tears in his eyes. *How the hell can I think about moving on?*

He headed farther north down Hwy B and saw more homes up for sale, but he drove past them. Maybe he was thinking too big right now. Maybe an apartment or loft would make the best choice for him.

Finally, after about another four miles and five turns, he found it—his new home.

CHAPTER TWO

The faded street sign said he was turning onto Jones Drive, and right at the end of the street, stood a vacant two-story white house. He could tell it was vacant because of its run-down condition, the fact that no cars were nearby, and because the one-car garage was empty—dirty, but empty. No other homes were on the street, which made this home perfect for him—he would enjoy the solitude. He felt it reaching for him like a force of nature. He pulled up to the house and got out of the Jeep with a smile on his face as he approached the front porch entrance. He looked around but didn't see a realtor sign, so he turned the knob and was pleased to find the door unlocked.

The foyer was bigger and nicer than he had expected. It needed lots of work, along with the rest of what he could see, but he was good with tools and certainly had the time on his hands. He flipped a switch and was surprised when the lights made a humming sound and flickered on. The faucet in the kitchen worked too. *It was shaping up to be his lucky day*. There was no furniture or dishes, so he would buy what he needed in the morning.

He unpacked the Jeep with a swag in his step and left the tools out so he could start right away. He would need to get lumber from the hardware store, but the sun was starting to set, so for the remainder of the evening, he took measurements. Then he rolled out his sleeping bag and went to bed for the night. At first, it was hard to fall asleep; it was so quiet there compared to the city. He focused on the sounds of the nearby wildlife. He could hear owls, crickets, frogs, and the howling of coyotes. Just as the pull of sleep finally overpowered him, though, he heard something else—it was a creaking door coming from upstairs.

CHAPTER THREE

Rhett woke with the sunlight streaming in from the cracked kitchen window. He rose, stretched, and added "windowpane" to his shopping list. He would need to find the hardware store and purchase lumber, paint, nails, and glass. There would probably be more to add to the list after he explored the house to check out its damage, but that would have to wait until after he had some coffee. That reminded him that he needed to make a list for his groceries too. He looked down at the filthy clothes he'd been wearing since yesterday. It was time to test out the shower after he downed his first cup.

The bathroom was on the second floor, and the pipes groaned when he turned the shower on. Rusty water came out first, so he waited until it ran clear and stepped inside. While lathering up, he heard a loud bang from downstairs and nearly jumped out of his skin. He didn't even bother to fully rinse off before hopping out of the shower and rushing downstairs in only his towel. His eyes scanned the living room first, and then he went into the kitchen, but he didn't see anyone. He walked back to the foyer and saw that the front door was bolted up just the way he'd left it. He descended the stairs to the basement, and the damp smell of mildew blanketed him. He would need to check for a leak, and there was no time like the present. He hadn't inspected the basement yet, so finding the ill-placed light switch was a chore. He flipped the switch, and the light buzzed and flickered before finally illuminating the dark shadows. The cellar had a tall, red tool chest and an abundance of cobwebs. He made a mental note to exterminate just as he heard music blaring from upstairs.

He took the steps two at a time while his heart thudded in his ears. The music was coming from the kitchen, and his radio was on the counter. He stared at it with his mouth gaping; he'd not even unpacked the radio yet let alone plugged it in. The back door was locked, and the porch was empty. Panic coursed through him with a cold trickle running down his spine. His body felt cold, yet his palms were sweating. He obviously wasn't alone, and he was still just wearing a towel. His eyes darted left then right as options ran through his mind. *Fight or flight?* He found the box marked "utensils," and he tore into it. He found the set of steak knives that he and Laura had received as a wedding gift and grabbed the largest one.

Rhett remained crouched like a tiger on the hunt as he crept to the living room entrance and paused. The knife shook uncontrollably in his hand, and he almost dropped it twice. He looked down at it and felt ashamed by his fear. *I'm a grown man for Christ's sake!* Nonetheless, he steadied the knife by gripping it in both hands, and just as he did, there was a distinct sound coming from upstairs—the sound of something heavy being dragged across the floor. His eyes darted to the stairs, and he found himself wishing he had his cell phone. But what would he do with it? Call the police? He was moving into the house illegally, so that would be an awkward conversation. No, he had to handle this by himself. Mustering as much courage as he could find, he tightened the towel, steadied the knife, and slowly ascended the stairs. His feet felt like lead weights as he took the steps one at a time. His breaths were loud and ragged, and he hoped he was the only one who could hear them. His knuckles were white from his grip on the quivering knife.

At the top of the stairs, all was dark, quiet, and eerie. The first room was a small bedroom on the right. Putting all his trust into the piece of cutlery, he slowly entered the darkened room and fumbled for the light switch—if he was going to be attacked, he wanted to face his attacker and look him dead in the eyes.

He looked around the empty room, which had a small window, chipped light-green paint, and some crayon markings on the walls, and then into the closet, which had a couple of wire hangers still hanging up inside—nothing. He turned the light off and continued down the hallway.

The next room was the bathroom on the left. Sunlight strained through the filmy, cracked window to illuminate the small room. He pushed aside the mildew-ridden shower curtain, even though he could see through it, and a spider scurried away.

The last room was the master bedroom. He braced himself before entering the quiet room, noticing that the air seemed unusually still, especially since he could hear the furnace rattling. Taking a deep breath, he steadied his grip on the knife and stepped forward. Then, from deep inside his chest, a grunted, "Hoowah," spewed forth, and he charged into the room with the knife raised by his head, ready to plunge—but it was empty except for a rusty queen-size bed frame.

He noticed the hatch to the attic because the pull rope was swinging. He had a couple of options at that point. He could go downstairs and put clothes on and then go up, or he could remain in his current vulnerable state and just go up. Either way, he had to finish what he'd started. *Shit*. He ran his free hand over his face. *I may as well just finish this.* He reached up and pulled the rope. There was a loud crack of wood, and a cloud of dust burst forth before the ladder fell forward. Choking on the dirt, he wiped his eyes and gripped the rungs to begin his climb. When he got to the top, he found himself enveloped in darkness and total quiet aside from his raspy wheezing. There was a window, which caught his eye, with a tiny beam of light struggling to peek through its small crescent shape. He gave his eyes a moment to adjust to the darkness, all the while listening for danger, and used that hopeful ray of light to look around. He could finally make out shapes of walls, shelving, and a trunk, but no humans. He finished his climb and fumbled his way through the shadows just to be sure. Nothing. He walked over to the trunk and tried to pry it open, but the antiquated lid wouldn't budge. He felt around and discovered its padlock. Relieved he was alone, but confused by it all, he turned to leave the way he came when something screeched and ran across his foot causing him to jump straight into the air and the towel to fall crumpled to the floor. Rats— he had rats. Rhett didn't consider himself a pussy by any means, but he drew the line at rodents in the dark. He shimmied down the rungs, pushed the ladder back up, and sealed the opening. Naked now, he walked back downstairs to get dressed while making a mental note to add rat traps to his shopping list.

He had no explanation for the radio or the noises he had heard, but all was calm now, and he had a lot to accomplish before it got dark. He brushed it off for the time being and took his clothes up to the master bedroom. He needed furniture, he thought as he looked around the empty room, so he had to make a trip into town. It was time for him to get acquainted with the locals.

CHAPTER FOUR

Rhett browsed through the living room sets at Wilson's Furniture Outlet first. He was perusing a beige sofa set when a petite brunette approached. Her nametag proclaimed she was Betty Hoff, and her overly enthusiastic smile told him that she worked on commission. Well, she'd be getting a fat one today.

"Good afternoon," she greeted him with an exuberant southern drawl. "I see you're admiring the Wade piece. It's one of our more popular selections," she gushed while running her hand over the back of the sofa as if she were petting it. "The fabric has Stain Guard, and it comes in four colors to choose from. Of course, we also have the rest of this showroom and another one downstairs we can look at too," she offered with a glimmer of hope to keep his interest in the store. "Now, before we begin to look around, may I have your name?"

"Sure, of course, where are my manners?" he answered sheepishly. "It's Rhett Shaw." He politely extended his hand and gave her a gentle shake.

"Do I detect a New York accent?" she inquired.

"Yeah," he said and nodded to emphasize. "I just moved here from Brooklyn."

"Well, welcome to the neighborhood. So, is the living room the only room you need to decorate?" He heard the quiet desperation in her voice. She needed this sale, and he didn't see a wedding ring on her finger, so he supposed that was one reason why. It was hard to make it on a single person's salary.

"No, actually, I need an entire house full of furniture. I'm redoing the entire place," he answered with a warm smile.

She didn't attempt to conceal her enthusiasm as her face beamed. "Well, you've come to the right place then, darlin'! We've got the best selections in town in our two-acre showroom."

Rhett looked down at his wristwatch. He still needed to go to the hardware and grocery stores, and he wanted to start repairs before it got dark out. "I tell you what," he began, "I'm in a hurry, so I'm going to have to pass on the full tour today."

Betty looked stunned. "But, but"—she shifted her weight nervously—"how you decorate and present your home is very important. You don't want to be stuck with something that creates bad Feng Shui."

He laughed lightly at the thought of someone trying to harmonize him with his environment. "It's all right. I'm not that picky. I just need a place to sit, eat, and sleep, and I'll be happy."

"But what about your family?" she asked with worry still etching her face. She was a pushy one indeed. "What about when company comes over?"

"Betty, I live alone, so no worries there, and I'm new in town, so I don't expect company to be dropping in. Just hook me up with something basic"—he stopped himself when he saw her face fall—"something *nice* for each room, and I'll be satisfied."

"Okay then, well"—she happily looked around at the massive showcase and clucked her tongue—"how about a matching recliner for the sofa to complete that set? Oh, and you'll want a coffee table for it of course." She spoke rapidly now—she was getting her game face on. "Step over here and take a look at what we just got in for the bedroom. It's a California King with a matching set of dressers and headboard."

"Wait," he exclaimed and held up a hand to stop her. He couldn't sleep in a king-size bed any longer. He hadn't slept in his bed back home since Laura died. "I want a twin or a queen-size."

"Oh"—she looked his lanky frame up and down—"if it's the difference in price, I know we have some discounted kings downstairs."

Rhett shook his head slowly. "No, it has nothing to do with that. Why don't you find me the perfect queen," he told her with a grin at his play on words.

"I can do that. Please follow me this way," she chirped and pointed to their left, where they walked just a few feet. "Now, this bed is a pillow top queen, and it also has a dresser set to match. It is going to be part of a promotion we are having next week if you want to wait." She looked up at him expectantly.

"No, that's okay. I'll take it now. You can have everything delivered today, can't you? I will pay extra if I need to." Money wasn't an issue for him. It wasn't because his book sales were so hot, although they had a steady pull of income. It was because Laura had signed them both up for one-million-dollar life insurance policies. She had thought living in a big city full of crime would be dangerous. Neither of them knew that an aneurism would be the predator to fear the most. Spending the money made him feel sick, though. It felt like dirty money. It was just another reminder that she wouldn't be coming home tonight.

"I'll have to check the schedule to see if the delivery boys are available, but if they are, there won't be a rush charge for getting it today." She clapped her palms together and rubbed. "There are plenty of other models to look at, so let's go downstairs." She pointed toward the northeast corner of the store.

He put his arm on hers and stopped her as she began to head in its direction.

"I tell you what"—he looked down at his watch—"I'm in a hurry, so I'm going to hire you to be my personal shopper. Just pick out what looks good and have it delivered today. I'll give you my credit card information and sign for it when they deliver." He quickly pulled his black MasterCard Diamond out of his wallet. "I assume that's okay?"

"I-I-I don't know. I mean it's not protocol, so I'll need to check with the manager, Mr. James," her voice quivered.

A voice boomed behind her then and made her jump. "I think we can accommodate Mister—" He looked quickly to Betty for the answer, but her attention was diverted toward a screaming child down another aisle. "I'm sorry you have me at a disadvantage here. I'm Jonah James, store manager, and you are?"

Rhett took the man's extended hand and gave it a firm shake. "Rhett Shaw. Nice to meet you."

"Welcome to Wilson's Furniture, Mr. Shaw. You know, if we don't have it, you don't need it," he said with a boom of laughter.

Rhett just smiled at the man's zealous advertising. "I'm sure she'll do just fine in selecting what I do need."

"Sure! Betty has a magnificent eye for style and for bargains too," he drawled. "And if you don't like it, we'll exchange it."

"I'm sure it will be fine. Now here's my card info"—Rhett handed the elite credit card over to Betty, and her hand shook a little when she took it—"Go ahead and make the charge, which I'll then sign for when it's delivered later this afternoon."

"Sure! The delivery boys will have everything there today by 6:00 sharp, and they'll help set it up too. We take care of our customers at Wilson's Furniture Outlet," the manager exclaimed.

"It all sounds great." Rhett emphasized his hurry by glancing at his watch and then the parking lot. "Now, I need to go if you're finished with me," he addressed Betty, who had just finished writing down his information.

"I'm all done. It will be my pleasure to help you out today, Mr. Shaw, and I do hope you admire my taste," Betty said while handing back his credit card.

"I'm sure I will. Now, I do really need to go, but feel free to add lamps, plants, or anything else you see that will be a good fit."

She squinted her eyes in confusion for a moment, and then recognition dawned upon her. "Oh, the plants are decoration for the store," she said with a sheepish grin.

"Well, if he wants the plants, we'll give him the plants," Mr. James chimed in.

Rhett extended his hand once more to wrap things up and gave them both a shake. "Thanks again."

His next stop was Jay's Hardware around the corner. The large store was tidy, so he had no problem with quickly finding the materials needed to start repairs on the fixer-upper, including some rat traps. Afterward, he popped into the IGA supermarket, which was two blocks down, to grab some groceries before making the trip home. *Home.* The word felt strange to him.

CHAPTER FIVE

Rhett first laid out the rat traps. Then he eagerly set about making some repairs. He had been a carpenter for fourteen years, so the repairs would be easy work for him; however, something about these repairs was oddly compelling. He felt an overpowering calmness as he began the renovations on the foyer's wooden floorboards, and when he started on the banister, he felt like an extension of the piece. He molded and sculpted the parched wood with new lumber where needed, carefully sanding out every knot. He ignored the splinters digging into his flesh as his hands ran over the length of the piece.

The radio, which *he* had turned on this time, blared his favorite hair bands from the kitchen—at least it had been. Now, heavy static came across, so he left his work area and went to check on it. By the time he got there, though, the problem, whatever it had been, corrected itself. *Oh well. When in Rome. . .* He grabbed a beer from the refrigerator and sauntered back to the foyer.

Whistling along to "Rock of Ages," Rhett reached for his hammer to finish nailing the revitalized banister in place, but he could only grasp air. It was gone. Feeling a little aggravated, he looked around the floor for where it must have fallen, but it wasn't there either. Now he was outright pissed.

"Damn it!" he spat over the music.

He'd left the hammer right there on the box of nails—he was sure of it. Yet here he was like a buffoon scouring the foyer. His eyes rested on a rag lying on the floor. It was out of place with his other rags because it was white, while they were blue. He rubbed his forehead out of frustration and kicked at the rag, soon regretting it because his big toe struck something hard.

"Fuck! Son-of-a-bitch!" he spewed forth with his fist waving in the air. The rag fell back and revealed the missing hammer lodged against a stack of lumber. "How in the hell?" he wondered aloud while bending over to pick it up.

He turned the tool over in his hands a couple of times before getting back to work. He hammered at the wood, making sure it was straight and sturdy, for twenty minutes before he decided to take a break. Cracking open another beer, he sat down to attempt to write a New York Times bestseller.

CHAPTER SIX

Rhett turned on his laptop and opened the manuscript for his third book, *The Edge of Reason.* Unfortunately, the Word document wasn't very large; he was only on chapter six and had no idea where he was going with the story. His editor would not be happy with him at their next meeting if he couldn't produce more—a lot more.

He closed his eyes and tried to picture his main characters. Set in Norfolk, Virginia—present day—there was his hero, Detective Rodney Small, who was investigating a string of murders, and there was Jack Harrison, the killer.

Rhett looked down at the cursor blinking on the screen; it was mocking him and taunting him to find the perfect things to say, the perfect set of words to whisk his audience away to the deepest corners of his imagination. When he'd written *Wolfsbane* and *Wolfsbane-the Blood of Dragons,* the ink had flowed at a comfortable pace that had appeased both his publisher and his fans. Lately, though, he felt dried up. It had been easy for him to use his imagination to write both of those stories, but this story was too real. He was going to be describing the kinds of events that actually happen.

He reread the scene on which he was stuck. In the scene, Detective Small was investigating the second murder to occur within a matter of days. He chewed his lip and thought about it for several minutes before an idea came to him. He put his fingers to the keyboard and typed, but he quickly erased the entire paragraph.

Frustrated, Rhett began to close the laptop lid, but when he touched it, it mysteriously shocked him. An electric tingle ran from his right shoulder down to his fingertips, which then began to fly across the keyboard as a new idea came to fruition. He had a crystal-clear vision in mind, and his words spilled forth like a tidal wave generating its own energy. The current pulled him forward as his thoughts formulated onto page after page, showing the vision in his mind's eye.

Rhett was in full swing, enjoying the sudden burst of productivity to its fullest, and almost didn't hear the knock on the front door. His brows stitched together in confusion as he rose from the rickety lawn chair, but then he remembered the delivery as he saw the space that would soon be some semblance of a comforting living room, and he smiled. He finally felt like things were looking up.

Forty-five minutes later, he had a house full of new furniture and accessories and was closing the front door behind the delivery men. Running his hand along the new railing, he took the stairs two at a time on the way to his bedroom to unpack his clothes into the new dressers and to put together his bed. A new bedspread and sheet set came with the mattress, so he unpacked it and made the bed up with tidy corners, which was something Laura had been a stickler for. Realizing what he had done, he thought about messing it up, but in the end, he left it. He looked at his watch; it was only 7:30, but he was tired, so he decided to take his shower, write a little more, and then go to bed.

After his refreshing wash, Rhett got clean boxers and a pair of shorts out of his new dresser. When he turned toward the new bed, though, he dropped them and wiped his eyes—the bed was a mess. The bedspread was bunched up, and the sheet was untucked. *Did I mess it up?* He knew he had thought about doing it, but he couldn't remember acting on it. He was still standing there naked, and given all that had already happened inside the house, he was feeling a little alarmed, but neither explained the deep chill that suddenly passed through him. It was a kind of cold that felt like the Grim Reaper was reaching into his chest and squeezing his heart. It was the kind of cold that made him pass out right there on the hardwood floor.

Rhett woke up confused, shivering, and with a pounding headache. He was lying naked on the bedroom floor, and when he looked up at the messy bed and gathered his wits about him, he remembered why—the bedding. He'd made the bed before his shower and someone, or something, messed it up. *No. That's foolish.* He had to have done it.

Shaking his head, he stood up with his boxers and shorts gathered in his left hand. He quickly dressed and hurried downstairs to check the thermostat, which read sixty-eight degrees.

He had completely overlooked the bloody handprint on the otherwise pristine blanket.

CHAPTER SEVEN

Rhett found a lap blanket in one of the unpacked boxes marked "hall closet," and he bundled himself up. He had no idea how long it would take the furnace to heat the house, but he had the feeling it would be a while. Out of the corner of his eye, he caught the cursor flashing on his laptop. It was a beacon of light calling out to him and saying the same old thing, "You should be writing," and he knew it was right. He grabbed a beer from the kitchen, sat down at his new desk, and got back to work.

He had left off in the story at the point when the first suspect was brought in for questioning. In the scene, Rodney had a gang banger in the interrogation room, and his temper was running hot.

Rhett's fingers barely even touched the keys as he rapidly typed. The words spilled forth like liquid from deep inside him and had no end in sight. They took him to places he hadn't even dreamed of going as he explored new dimensions with his characters. He must've gotten sleepy, though, because he found himself waking up with the sun shining brightly in his eyes, and he was still at his desk.

With a crick in his neck, he looked around the room and felt out of sorts—again. The laptop was still on, and he saw that he'd made a lot of progress with the story. Wiping the sleep from his eyes, he rose from the chair, stretched out his cramped muscles, and then headed into the kitchen to start the coffee. His cell phone was on the kitchen counter, and it flashed three missed calls—all from Dave Sage, his editor. *Odd.* He checked the ringer, and the volume was on full blast, but he hadn't heard it. It must have been while he was passed out, but he normally didn't sleep that soundly. He knew he should call him back immediately, but he didn't feel like dealing with him right then. With his coffee in hand, he opened the back door, which creaked in pain on its rusty hinges, and stepped out onto the small back porch. The early morning air was cool and refreshing as it hit his face, which brought to his attention the fact he needed to turn the thermostat back down a little. There was a light fog creeping across the lawn and surrounding woods, but it looked like it was going to be a sunny day.

He set his coffee mug down on the porch railing and looked down at his phone. *No time like the present.* He swiped across the screen to unlock it and pressed the button to access his nearly empty phonebook, but then the screen froze and flashed an incoming call—it was Dave beating him to the punch.

"Dave, I was just trying to call you," he explained.

"I'm sure you were," the editor grumbled. "You've been ducking my calls, which must mean you don't have anything for me." It wasn't a question, it was an accusation, and it was loud and clear.

"Actually, I do. I have several chapters I can send you," Rhett promised.

"While I appreciate the fact that you've made some progress, I was hoping you'd be sending a *book* over," Dave countered.

Rhett found himself growing irritated with the man's pushing. "Well, when I have a book, you'll be the first to know," he snapped. "It's practically writing itself now; I can tell you that," he continued and then wondered how odd it was that that was true. It did seem to be writing itself. He heard a disgruntled sigh and added more politely this time, "I'll send what I have now and let you know when I have more. Now let me get back to work. Later, Dave." The phone went dead, and he just held it in his palm staring at it. It wasn't like him to lose his temper like that.

Grabbing his coffee, he went back inside and flicked on the radio. A newscaster was going on about the nice weather in store for the area that day, but then his voice turned grim as he announced that a local woman, who was a gun and pawn shop owner, had been murdered the previous night. Police reported that an intruder broke into her shop while she was closing, stabbed her multiple times, and broke into the gun case. A Colt Python 357 Magnum revolver, along with money from the register, had been reported missing by the victim's husband.

Rhett closely listened to the details of the crime—something sounded familiar, but his head was a little foggy yet. He poured another cup of coffee and paced the kitchen in a path around the unpacked boxes. He added that to his mental list of things to do for the day—he'd unpack, do some further repairs, and try to find the time and inspiration to write. *That's it!* He took long strides into the living room and sat at his desk. The laptop was in sleep mode, so he woke it up and entered his password. There it was on the pages in front of him—his crime scene was a small store where a woman was stabbed to death, and a gun was stolen. Rhett chewed his bottom lip.

"No fucking way," he said aloud. "Am I suddenly clairvoyant?"

He got up to get some aspirin from one of the boxes before going upstairs to get dressed to start working on the repairs. He decided he'd start on the porch today; he'd noticed some loose floorboards, and the railing needed some fixing up as well.

He grabbed a T-shirt and some jeans out of the dresser and tossed the shirt onto the bed before stepping into the pants. When he picked the shirt up, though, he discovered a bloody handprint on his otherwise snow-white blanket. His eyes flew to his hands, which he turned over and inspected carefully for cuts. He found an abrasion on his palm, which he couldn't account for, but it wasn't deep. He didn't think it could have bled enough to create the handprint on the bed, but then again, there was no other explanation. A startling knock on the front door made him quickly don the shirt as he headed that way.

He took the stairs two at a time and then looked through the glass window on the front door. A woman with short blonde hair was standing on the porch and messing with her smartphone. He opened the door, and when she looked up, his first thought was *damn*. The attractive woman, who appeared to be in her twenties, smiled broadly.

"Hi there. I'm wondering if you can help me," she said with a slight drawl. "I went for a drive in the country, and I think I'm lost now."

He stared into her mesmerizing green eyes and returned her warm smile. "I'm new to the area, so I don't know how much help I can be." Her face fell, so he quickly added, "But I'll try." He held his right hand out to her and said, "I'm Rhett, by the way."

She looked at his hand cautiously before accepting it. "Hi, Rhett, I'm Bridget. It's nice to meet you."

He noticed her dimples this time when she smiled. She was undisputedly attractive. "Nice to meet you," he responded in kind. "I'd invite you in"—he gestured over his shoulder—"but as I said, I just moved in, and the place is a wreck. I'm renovating it, though," he explained.

"That's okay," she murmured. "Would you happen to have a map in your possession? I can't get a decent signal on my phone to use Google."

"You know what? I don't think I do, but we can use my computer to access Google Maps. So, screw the mess. Would you like to come in?" he asked with a grin.

Her face lit up, and she nodded. "Sure." She followed him inside the house and to his desk.

He minimized his Word document and opened up a new tab in the browser. "Here we go," he said while clicking the mouse and bringing up a location search box. "I notice a slight accent. Are you new to the area too?" He looked up and caught her smiling down at him.

She quickly looked away and lowered her lashes. "Yes, I am. I'm here from South Carolina visiting my cousin. She had to work today, though, so I thought I'd go for a drive in the country, but I think I went too far," she explained. "I was following a truck when I found myself here." She shrugged and eyed the computer screen.

"Okay, well, where do you need to get back to? Where does she live?"

"She lives in Bennington on 4th Street. And... umm...her house number is 108."

"All right," he murmured while typing in the address. "Here we go. It says you are 6.7 miles east of her house. That's not too far."

The information made her smile, but then her expression changed. She turned and looked at the staircase in the foyer. "Is someone upstairs? Do you have a family?" She had a slight look of disappointment gracing her pretty face.

Rhett squinted his gray eyes and frowned at her. "Umm, no, it's just me. Why do you ask?"

"Oh, because I could swear I heard hushed voices coming from upstairs." She looked over her shoulder at the darkened stairwell and shrugged.

"Hmm, well, like I said, it's just me. I'll print this map out for you, and then I need to get going myself. I need to buy some more wood from the hardware store, so I can work on my porches." He stood up and grabbed his car keys from the coffee table nearby while handing her the printed map.

"Thanks. I need to get going as well. I promised to start dinner before Beth got home from work"—she looked down at her watch— "Looks like I'll barely make it in time." She gave a lighthearted chuckle.

He walked her out to her car, making small talk along the way. She told him that she taught second grade, and he told her about his writing.

"Thank you so much for helping me, and I promise to look up your books."

He smiled sheepishly. "You don't have to, but that would be great. I can always use another fan."

"Perfect and maybe I'll bring it by for an autograph," she hinted.

His face fell. There was no way he was ready for interaction like that—this was a stretch for him already. "Umm, sure, if you want to. Now, I have to go get the lumber and get to work on the porch while there's still light out. It was nice to meet you." He knew his words had been rushed, and that made him feel a little foolish and self-conscious, but he felt an overwhelming desire to quickly get out of there.

"Oh, well, I understand," she said softly on a disappointed sigh. "Umm, thanks again." She gave him a little wave and climbed into her Taurus.

As he drove to the hardware store, Rhett thought about the whispering Bridget said she'd heard. In truth, he'd heard it too.

CHAPTER EIGHT

Rhett purchased the lumber and other supplies he needed and worked hard on the porch while the last rays of sunlight flickered through the rustling trees. The air was thick and humid, and he could smell rain on a gust of wind.

"Ouch, goddamnit!" he hollered as the hammer came down on this left thumb. "Son-of-a-bitch!"

He rubbed the injured digit, but that seemed to make it worse. Even in the creeping darkness, he could see the blood welling up underneath the nail, turning it black. Having been a carpenter before, he was no stranger to this kind of injury, but that didn't make it hurt less. Indeed, each time felt worse than the last, and he dreaded what he needed to do.

He went into the house, grabbed a lighter, and let the flame flicker all around the tip of his pocketknife. When he was satisfied that it was sterilized, he took a seat at his desk. He put his thumb flat on the desk and began to carve a small hole in the nail—it was the only way to relieve some of the God-awful throbbing.

"Fuck!" he spat as the pain radiated up his arm, and blood bubbled up from under the nail. He gave it an excruciatingly painful squeeze to get enough blood out to make enough difference. Thankfully, it was working.

As he dabbed away at the blood with a tissue, he shivered. He wasn't sure if it was from the needle-like pain or the sudden cold draft he felt, but it made him look up and all around himself. Of course, nothing was there, but he thought he felt *something*.

Grabbing the clip-on light he'd bought at the lumberyard, he went back to work on the porch. He was extra careful, though, not to mash any other fingers. It was a few minutes past 9:00 when he decided to call it quits for the day. There was always tomorrow.

He sat down at the desk with a ham sandwich and a beer and stared at the cursor blinking on the laptop screen. He still felt blocked. He reread his work from earlier, editing a few things, and then started to type. He ended up deleting it, though, and then racked his brain to think up the next crime his character would commit. Rhett closed his eyes and tried to step into his character's shoes.

Jack Harrison, the killer, was a twenty-year-old product of the juvenile system. He had been in several foster homes since the age of three, and most of them were not good. He had been abused—mentally, physically, and sexually—by a couple of his caregivers. *Caregivers?* That word meant nothing to him. No one cared. Ever. Now, living in a one-bedroom economy apartment—infested with rodents and roaches—he had time to think, and he thought a lot. He thought about revenge mostly. He also thought about how to get out of that place—Norfolk, Virginia.

What would his next move be? What did he need the most, and how would he get it? Rhett answered his thoughts aloud, "Money. He needs money, and now he has a gun to get it."

Rhett began to type slowly as the words formed on the tip of his tongue, and then he typed faster as complete thoughts took shape.

GET
OUT

Jack bought a ski mask from the dollar store nearby before knocking off a small gas station on the other side of town. The ski mask wasn't a telltale purchase since it was the middle of January, so there was nothing about that to make him stand out. The gas station had only one attendant, and it only took a bullet between the eyes to shut him up. He could have let the man live since he was wearing the mask, but the fellow looked like one of his foster fathers, and that bastard didn't deserve to live. Unfortunately, there was only a couple hundred dollars in the cash register, so he'd have to plan on another hit, but it wouldn't be tonight.

Tonight, he'd go to a bar and celebrate with a drink. He'd grown up in homes of abusive alcoholics, so he never really developed a taste for the stuff; however, a good bourbon was called for on occasion. Thankfully, he was never carded—his hard life made him look much older than he was. That way, too, no one could identify him by his real name.

A pretty Latina was making fuck-me eyes at him by his second drink, so he offered to buy her one too. Then one became two, and two became three. She was a lightweight, so she was in no condition to get herself home by that point. He offered her a ride to the motel she was holing up in while she looked for a new apartment. She'd been babbling on about a recent breakup with her boyfriend and said he kicked her out or something like that. Jack was too busy admiring her perky tits to pay much attention. After all, she had them on display in a tight, low-cut top. In the motel room, though, she had them in full view as she sidled up to him.

"Come here, big boy," she slurred in what she probably thought was a seductive voice. "I know you like what you see," she added when he didn't make a move.

It wasn't that she wasn't attractive; it was just that the alcohol fumes coming off her reminded him of Bill, his worst foster father, and the memory was making him angrier by the second. *This little slut needs to pay.* He led her to the bed, removed her thigh-high stockings, and used them to tie her wrists up. She thought it was a sex game and started to laugh. Her non-stop giggling was infuriating and added fuel to the fire.

"Are you ready?" he murmured in her right ear.

"Oh yeah," she slurred.

"Here it comes," he said in a voice that made her eyes bulge because it wasn't a welcoming tone, and it wasn't sexy.

He could see she was instantly regretting her decision to invite him in, but she didn't even know why yet. That amused him. He slowly took out his pocketknife and held it close to her right eye. She began to squirm wildly on the bed, and tears sprang forth as she tried to scream. His hand was too fast, though, and he covered her mouth to stifle her scream into a quiet whimpering.

"I'd hold still if I were you. The blade is awfully close," he taunted, and she stopped moving so wildly.

He unexpectedly grabbed her hair and tugged it tight before lopping some of it off with the knife. She was still scared, he could tell, but relief washed over her. He couldn't have that.

He slapped her hard with his free hand and growled, "You're a bad girl. You've been bad, and you need to be taught a lesson."

He took the knife and sliced down her right wrist to the middle of her forearm. Then he did the other arm as well. He made sure to cut down to the bone until he heard the knife scrape.

She began convulsing. Her eyes rolled back into her head, and her body bucked wildly on the squeaky bed. She was going into shock. He ended it, though, with a quick plunge of his knife into her stomach.

Jack washed up in the tiny motel room bathroom and left with his trinket—her lock of hair. He smiled the entire drive back home. Murdering the bitch from the secondhand store had just been because she'd surprised him while he was making off with the gun, but this, this was fun. Punishing people was fun.

Rhett leaned back in his chair feeling very satisfied. Yes, Dave would be happy with him once he got this chapter. Maybe it would even get the editor off his back for a while.

He was still mentally celebrating his work when he heard a loud creaking noise, which he at first assumed was the floorboard moaning from the weight of the chair, but then there was a loud slam from a door. That sound distinctly came from upstairs, and now his heart raced.

He pulled out his pocketknife again and quietly treaded the staircase. The door to the small bedroom was closed. Mustering up as much courage as he could, he slowly opened the door and flicked on the light with his left hand. Nothing. He approached the closet, but it was just as it had been. *What the fuck?* He checked the bathroom and master bedroom, but they too were empty. *Am I going mad?* That had to be it. But then again, Bridget had heard noises earlier as well. He dismissed the closed door as a result of being in a drafty old house. Even now, he could hear the furnace hissing as it struggled to force air through the vents.

"Well, shit," he exclaimed aloud and trotted back downstairs to do some more work on his book.

When he sat down to write, though, he couldn't shake the feeling that he was being watched. He looked around the room, searching every dark corner, scrutinizing every shadow. Suddenly, his phone rang and made him jump out of the chair. It was Dave calling again.

"Hey, Dave, did you receive the chapters?" he questioned with child-like enthusiasm.

"Yes, I got them. It's pretty good, but I was hoping for more than that," Dave griped.

Rhett let out an exasperated sigh. "Rome wasn't built in a day, Dave."

"Rhett, you aren't my first or only client. I know it takes time; I just wish you'd pick up the pace. You are one hell of an author, and I want this book to be on the shelves by next spring."

Rhett gave a light chuckle. "I will do my best. Now is that all? I'd like to get back to it."

"Yeah, I suppose that's all for now. See if you can't pound out another couple of chapters tonight. See ya." The line went dead.

"Humph, easier said than done," Rhett uttered while going into the kitchen for a beer. Deciding against it, he got a glass of water instead. The unfiltered water tasted horrible, though, so he reached for a can of Pepsi. When he popped the tab, the beverage foamed over and sprayed at him. It was the normal result after shaking a can, but he'd barely moved it. *What the hell is going on around here?*

After cleaning up the mess, he sat back down at his laptop. He didn't go back to working on his book, though. Instead, he began to run a Google search about parapsychology, but before the search was finished, he heard a loud crack, felt a sharp sting to his head, and then everything went black.

CHAPTER NINE

Rhett came to in a whirl of pain. "Argh," he moaned as his hand flew to his throbbing head wound. He felt moisture and could smell the metallic scent of blood. Sure enough, there was some on his fingertips when he pulled them away.

He searched around the area to see what had hit him. On the floor, in a million tiny shards of glass, was a shattered light fixture. He looked up at the ceiling and saw the crack leading to where the light had been and the wires sticking out of the opening. Shaking his head in dismay, he mentally added it to his list of things to repair. He looked at his laptop, which thankfully was untouched by the light. The cursor blinked on a blank search engine page. Rhett squinted his eyes and grimaced because he couldn't remember what he had been doing, especially through the haze of pain.

He sat down to work on the book, but with a yawn, he realized it was already after 11:00. *I was out for a long time.* His hand went to his head again, and he felt the stickiness, along with a sizable lump. He could tell that the blood was drying up because his fingertips felt crust. With a slow shake of his pounding head, he fetched two more aspirin before trudging up the stairs to his bedroom. He didn't walk past the small bedroom without first looking inside. Still nothing.

He undressed down to his boxer shorts and started to climb underneath the blanket. Before turning out the light, however, he wanted to get another look at the bloody handprint, for which he still couldn't account. It was gone. The cozy blanket was an immaculate white. His eyes bulged, and blood rushed to his ears as he jumped out of the bed and flipped the blanket over to its other side. Spotless white. With a racing heart, he scanned the sheet, just in case he was confused earlier, but it was also perfectly clean. His hands flew to his head and ran through his thick hair and over the lump. He was so confused. His eyes darted all around the room, from the ceiling to the floor, and back again.

"I'm losing my mind; it's the only explanation," he admitted aloud to himself. He decided the only thing to do was to seek professional help. He needed a shrink.

Sleep was fitful that night when it finally came to him. He started to dream about Laura. She was walking away from him in a field of daisies, and he ran to catch up to her while shouting her name. He was out of breath by the time she slowed down, so he couldn't talk. He could only reach out and tap her shoulder, but when she turned around, it wasn't her. It was something he would have seen only in the goriest horror movie. Her once flawless face was old, ancient in fact, and withered with bone showing through and bugs crawling out of the empty eye sockets. Her mouth was in the form of a snarl, and a gurgling erupted as she reached out and pointed an accusing finger, which was nothing but bone, at him. Rhett found his voice and screamed.

He shot up in the bed with sweat pouring down his face in rivulets and his breath coming in gasps. He'd never had such a terrible dream before, and he just couldn't fathom why it involved his sweet wife.

He didn't want to go back to sleep, but after forty minutes of tossing and turning, he couldn't keep his eyes open any longer. More bad dreams came to him. He dreamed about Laura being trapped inside a burning house while he watched helplessly from the front yard. He tried to get to the garden hose, but it was as if his feet were in cement, and every step he managed to take sent him backward two steps. He stood there helpless while the love of his life burned in the fires of hell. He'd never felt less of a man.

CHAPTER TEN

Rhett didn't feel rested at all the next morning, but he was glad to see the sun peeking in through the tears in his window shade. He rubbed the sleep out of his eyes and padded to the bathroom to face that familiar morning problem—pissing with morning wood.

He started the shower and climbed in just as soon as the water changed from tepid to hot. He was only in a couple of minutes, though, when it turned ice cold. He jumped out, toweled off, dressed, and headed to the basement to check the water heater. He popped out the element and found it was corroded, so he added that to his mental list of repairs for the day. It meant another trip into town, which he didn't relish.

He trudged back up the stairs and took hold of the doorknob, but it wouldn't turn. He figured it was just stuck, so he went back down the stairs to his tool chest and grabbed a can of WD-40. Even after spraying on a liberal amount, though, the knob wouldn't budge. It was locked. He scanned the door and the knob while his mind's eye scanned the other side. The lock on it was like the others inside the house—it required the turn of a skeleton key to lock it. So, of course, there's no way to lock oneself in. Also, just to further complicate the situation, he recalled with one hundred percent clarity that there had been no key in the lock, to begin with.

Not knowing what to think, other than the fact that he needed to get on the other side of that door, he ran back down the stairs and over to the workbench. He pushed it beneath a small window that looked big enough to accommodate his slender form. He flipped its lock, which required more effort than it should have, and pushed upward, but it wouldn't budge. He used both hands and tried again, but it didn't move at all. Feeling utterly frustrated and desperate, he used a nearby hammer and shattered it. Luckily, most of the glass exploded outward. He brushed away what was on his clothing and stacked a couple of crates on top of the workbench.

He climbed up on the crates and pushed himself through the window, which was a tight fit. He still had the hammer in hand to use as a weapon against the intruder. *How else could the door have been locked?*

But something nagged at him. Assuming someone was in the house, where did they find the key? He didn't even know where one was. He had installed a brand-new lock on the front door since he hadn't found any keys. After all, the house was abandoned. *Or was it?*

It occurred to him that maybe somebody came back home. A chill ran down his spine. He didn't know what to expect on the other side of the front door, and the dreadful possibilities rattled his bones.

He reached above the doorframe for the spare key. After unlocking the door, he slowly turned the knob and cringed when it produced a loud squeak. To pump himself up, he thought about Jack. What would his antagonist do in this situation? *He wouldn't be afraid of anyone.* Feeling more aggressive now that he was in character, he stepped inside. He didn't hear anything other than the sound of shutters banging up against the house in the morning wind and his own creaky footsteps, which seemed to echo off the walls. He searched every corner of the main floor and then the upstairs area, but no one was there.

Scratching his head in confusion, he went back downstairs where he saw something that temporarily made his heart stop and slam against his chest wall—the basement door was wide open.

Clearly, someone is fucking with me. The logic seemed reasonable, but it didn't shake the cold terror gripping him even as sweat ran down his forehead. Slowly, he approached the door. He closed it and examined the lock. The keyhole was still empty, but then something caught his eye. There was something dark lying on the floor in the corner. He bent to pick it up—it was a skeleton key.

"That still doesn't explain how the door locked. The key wasn't in the hole, and in any case, it couldn't turn itself," he argued with himself, and more shivers tickled his spine. He urgently locked the door and put the key into his pocket.

Rhett glanced at his watch. It was already after 9:00, and he still had a lot of work to do on the house, including going to the hardware store for the heating element. He'd also need to replace the basement window now. He grabbed his set of keys and cell phone off the coffee table and stepped outside. As he turned the key in the lock, he was certain he heard laughter coming from inside the house. It was high-pitched and childlike, but it still made his skin crawl. *No one is inside the house—I checked. It has to be coming from outside.* He looked down the empty street to see if children were playing somewhere nearby, perhaps on the adjoining street, but there was nary a soul. He shook his head and once again considered calling a psychiatrist.

Perhaps if he'd looked up, he would've seen the eyes watching him from the upstairs window.

CHAPTER ELEVEN

Rhett returned home an hour later with a new heating element and a new basement window. He'd also purchased multiple cans of paint. He would repaint the outside white with red trim and the bedrooms blue. He bought a cheery yellow shade for the bathroom because yellow had been Laura's favorite color. He almost chose another shade, but he wanted to keep pieces of her alive and in view.

He looked around the yard as he unloaded the Jeep. After the house was finished, he would need to tackle it. Grass seed needed to be put out, and it could also use a flowerbed in the front. The backyard blended into the woods, so he would just plant more grass. This meant, of course, he would need to buy a lawnmower before too long.

The spring afternoon was warm, and beads of sweat formed across his forehead while he carried his purchases inside. Just as he stepped inside the foyer, droplets of perspiration dripped into his eyes and caused them to burn. He dropped the paint he'd been holding in his right hand and reached for the bottom of his T-shirt to wipe the sweat away. Before he wiped, though, he saw something at the top of the stairs. It was blurry through his tears, but he was sure there was something there—something that was glowing. He stared, ignoring the persistent burning in his eyes, and gradually, the translucent glow took on human shape. Frantically, he used his shirt bottom to wipe the sweat and tears away. He looked back up and saw only the shadowed landing. He dropped the other paint can and took the stairs two at a time. He was sure he'd seen someone.

He looked inside the small bedroom, the bathroom, and his bedroom, but they were empty. He grabbed a flashlight and pulled down the attic ladder. At the top, he stayed on the ladder while shining the light all around the space. The light glinted off dozens of cobwebs and piles of junk, which he had yet to go through, but it didn't find anyone. *Shit! I'm losing my fucking mind!* Since he was there anyway, he climbed the rest of the way up and checked the rat traps. There was one captured rodent, so he carefully picked the trap up at its ass end, even though the creature was dead, and descended the ladder. He carried the critter to the woods and tossed it in while it was still in the trap. He'd forgotten to buy garbage cans, and he would need a couple soon. He didn't know what the trash pick-up days were, so he'd just leave it outside and wait. Hopefully, they'd see it from the main road and know to start collecting again. He had no idea how long the house had been vacant.

When he got back inside, he picked up the heating element and turned toward the basement, but an eerie feeling stopped him. He'd had enough of the dank cellar for one day; however, he knew he would need a shower after doing more repairs, so he continued walking on wobbly legs in its direction. He tried the knob, but it wouldn't turn. Then he remembered that he'd locked it, so he pulled the key out of his pocket and unlocked the door. He left it open this time and walked down the stairs. When he flipped on the lights, they made their usual hum before flickering on, but they took a little longer this time. He would need to buy light bulbs to fit all the fixtures in the house on his next trip into town. That made him think about the electric bill. He'd need to contact the electric company to put it in his name, or he might find himself in complete darkness soon. He shuddered when he thought about being in the dark inside *this* house.

It took him about thirty minutes to change the heating element, and he only cut himself once. It was a good thing he'd already had a tetanus shot because the old element was rusted out. He cleaned his tools up and went back upstairs, feeling relieved when he saw the door was still wide open.

His eyes scanned the foyer and the lumber lying there. He told himself that he should keep the momentum going and do more repairs on the porch, but he felt inspired to write. So, after he washed his hands in the kitchen, he fixed a ham sandwich, grabbed a Pepsi, and sat at his laptop. He took a bite of the sandwich while the laptop warmed up. It encouraged him to download the latest Windows updates, so he told it to go ahead and install them. He'd have his lunch in the meantime.

He took another healthy bite of the sandwich, but it got stuck in his throat, choking off his air supply. He clutched the edge of the desk with his left hand, and his right went to his throat. He gasped for air with his lungs on fire, and his heart felt like it would burst from his chest while he desperately sought a solution to his dilemma. He tried convulsing his esophagus to force the food back up, but it wasn't working, so he made a fist and punched himself hard in the stomach. Surprisingly, it worked, and the chunk of food flew out and across the floor.

Once he regained his composure and cleaned up the mess, Rhett realized something he'd been unable to pay attention to a few minutes ago. While he'd been choking on the food, he'd heard the childish laughter again.

He stepped outside onto the run-down porch and looked all around. He still didn't see any children. He didn't see anybody at all.

Since his imagination was already running wild, he decided to put it to beneficial use. His laptop was done updating, and he was ready to write.

CHAPTER TWELVE

It was Saturday in his story, and Jack had just woken up. He found the lock of hair he'd lopped off on his nightstand, and a broad smile crossed his lips. He replayed the night before like a horror movie in his mind. Her high-pitched whimpers still rang in his ears, and the image of her bulging eyes was crystal clear. He needed to feel that rush again—soon.

After downing a bowl of dry cereal, he took a shower and got the rest of the Latina's blood out from under his fingernails. He dressed, stuffed the gun and his knife into his pockets, and left the disgusting apartment.

The January morning was freezing, but his baggy hoodie kept some of the frigid air out. He couldn't afford a winter coat, so the hoodie made do. His fingers twitched as he looked up and down the street. His neighborhood wasn't a welcoming one. It wasn't a part of Norfolk people wanted to visit, let alone live in, but it's all he could afford. The only work he could find lately was as a janitor, cleaning business offices, and it didn't pay enough. The good thing about it, though, was that he got to work independently. He couldn't stand the idea of a boss constantly looking over his shoulder or co-workers rambling on about their mundane lives.

Whenever he was cleaning an office, his wandering eyes liked to go through interoffice mail and company files. He learned when people were getting fired before they did, and that provided him with sick pleasure.

He had a list of credit card numbers tucked away under his twin mattress at home. He'd taken them from a couple of companies who provided automatic billing to their customers. He used them sparingly and only a few times each so it wasn't obvious to the owners. He figured that people who were wealthy enough to pay the high interest rates on credit cards probably didn't spend too much time examining their statements when they came in the mail. He could only use those card numbers for phone orders, but he often picked pockets and snatched purses, too, so he had a couple of physical cards for in-store purchases.

Agnes Coleman's was one he liked to use. He always told the store clerks that she was his mother and was unable to leave the house because of her disabilities. He was just running her errands like a good soon should.

Luckily, the elderly woman hadn't remembered to cancel the card. She probably just dutifully paid it off each month using her husband's retirement pension.

Jack decided he needed a new thrill today. It wasn't fun when his crime sprees were too easy and predictable. Yes, robbing the gas station and killing the clerk had been amusing, but it wasn't enough.

He climbed into his junky Toyota Camry, which he'd traded some of the credit card data for, and began to drive down Washington Avenue. The car made a rattling noise as it puttered along, but at least it got him from point A to point B.

Today, point B was a car title loan business ran by one lonely worker. Jack had spent numerous days watching the business to see how much traffic it received and the times of day it was busiest.

He fingered the ski mask in his hoodie pocket with a malicious grin and parked around the backside of the building. He put on the ski mask and picked the lock on the back door, holding his breath when the door's alarm went off.

The woman operating the office rushed his way with a gun in her trembling hands. However, his Colt was already pointed in her direction, so it made her hesitate. He pulled back on the hammer, causing an audible click, and her hand trembled even more until she dropped her weapon. He knew she didn't have it in her to fire the gun at him. It probably wasn't even loaded.

He laughed and told her, "That's right. You don't want to go there with me. Now, lock the front door and give me the cash."

Trembling so much that she almost fell, the woman walked to the door and turned the deadbolt. The only sound in the room was her soft whimpering until the click of the heavy lock rang out. She wobbled her way to the safe and withdrew all the cash, which she dropped once before handing it over to Jack.

"Clumsy thing today, aren't you?" he sneered.

Through sobs, she sniveled, "Please, take the money and leave."

Jack looked the woman up and down. Her nonstop trembling escalated his excitement. He considered assaulting her, but he saw someone pulling into the parking lot. He grabbed her by the wrist and pulled her to the back of the office. He struck her across the cheek, causing her to fall to the floor. Then he held the gun above her as he stared into her distorted face. He grabbed her matching blazer, which was hanging on a coat rack, wadded it up, and held it against her temple. Then he pressed the gun's muzzle into it and pulled the trigger. His homemade silencer wasn't perfect, but it muffled the noise enough. He took the blood-stained jacket with him when he left. His trinket collection was growing, but it wasn't big enough yet.

GET
OUT

Rhett saved his work and sat back with a smile. *This should make Dave happy.* He looked at his watch, noting that it was already after 1:00. He still had a lot of work to do on the house, so he turned off the laptop, grabbed his hammer and some lumber, and went back to the front porch to finish replacing the floorboards and railing.

He finished replacing the floorboards by 4:30 and decided to take a break for supper. Sweat was dripping down his face again, so he quickly mopped it up with a rag to avoid burning his eyes this time. He went to the kitchen and grabbed a can of chicken noodle soup out of the flimsy cupboard. It was just one more thing that needed fixing. In fact, all the cabinets needed renovating or replacing. He looked around the small kitchen and couldn't help but think that for a free house, it was certainly costing him some money. He put the bowl of soup into the microwave and set the timer for three minutes. While it heated, he stepped onto the back porch and observed all the work it needed to have done. It would probably have to wait until the inside of the house was finished. After he ate his soup, he'd work more on the living room area tonight. The flooring needed replacing, which would involve sanding and varnishing the lumber he'd bought.

While enjoying his soup, in slow bites so he didn't start choking again, he pulled up Netflix on his laptop. He would have to call the local internet provider to have his service set up soon. Running on a generous neighbor's open Wi-Fi access was a risky gamble, especially in his line of work. He wasn't planning on ordering cable television, though. He didn't watch much TV anymore, and what he did watch could be found on Netflix or somewhere online. Now, he searched through the westerns available to watch. He chose a John Wayne movie, and a smile played across his lips. Every time he used to turn on a western, Laura would roll her eyes and comment that she didn't know that she'd married a cowboy. Cuddling up with her to watch old-time movies had always been moments to cherish, and he longed to have them back.

He was in the middle of a bite of soup when a crash sounded from upstairs. "Shit!" he yelped as the hot broth spilled down his front. He quickly dabbed at the burning mess on his shirt and then ran up the stairs. In his bedroom, his change jar had fallen off his dresser; although, there was no logical reason for it. He was certain it had been in the middle of the dresser top, and there wasn't a strong enough breeze from the vent to blow it off, so...*I swear, I think I'm not alone.*

He put the jar in the top dresser drawer this time and went back to his meal and the movie. *It's a good thing I'm not into scary movies.*

As soon as the movie ended, Rhett took another shower and went to bed. As he lay on his side, though, a strange feeling made the hairs stand up on his neck. He felt like someone was watching him—again.

CHAPTER THIRTEEN

Rhett woke up from a leg cramp as the first rays of light were peeking in through his window. He quickly climbed out of bed and pressed his full weight on the leg to relieve the spasm. When the pain finally subsided, he put on a clean T-shirt and a pair of jeans and headed into the bathroom to take care of his morning business.

He rinsed the remnants of shaving cream from his face and looked up into the mirror. His heart thudded inside his chest—it wasn't just his reflection he was seeing. He spun on his heel, prepared to defend himself with nothing but his razor in hand; however, there was no one there. He bolted through the doorway and scanned the empty corridor in complete confusion while trying to remember how to breathe. Then he rubbed his dry eyes. They must be so tired that they caused him to see something that wasn't there. *How could someone be there?*

"That's it; I'm for sure looking up the local shrinks," he said aloud, descending the staircase.

As he crossed the foyer, he heard a thud against the front door and jumped. He flung it open and found a neatly folded up newspaper lying on the porch.

"The previous residents must have been subscribers," he told himself.

He took the paper with him into the kitchen to start the coffee. While it brewed, he stepped out onto the back deck and flipped the paper open. On the front page, there was an article about a murder that occurred the day before. The office manager for a local title loan company was found shot to death in the locked building. So far, the police had no suspects.

Rhett stared wide-eyed at the words in utter disbelief while clenching his clammy hands. He had a suspect for them, but it was a fictional character from his story. Once had been a bizarre coincidence, but twice—that was just unbelievable. He turned to go inside to call the police, even though he had no idea what to say to them, but wooziness suddenly overpowered him. He felt his air supply choke off, and everything went black.

He came to, and his head was pounding with the strength of one hundred jackhammers. He blinked his eyes and looked around the porch in confusion, not remembering even going out there.

"What the hell was I doing?" he asked aloud while massaging the lump on his head.

He looked to his side and saw a piece of guttering. *Oh. It must've fallen and struck me.* He slowly stood and went inside to make some coffee. He quickly saw, though, that the coffee was already brewed. He squinted his eyes at the black liquid and tried to piece together the morning hours. He had no idea how long he'd been up.

CHAPTER FOURTEEN

Rhett opened his email to find a lengthy message from Dave. He raved about the chapters and encouraged Rhett to keep up the good writing but at a faster pace.

"Way to turn a compliment around, Dave," he mumbled.

The rest of his inbox was junk, so he deleted those messages. Drumming his fingers on the desk, he opened a new browser tab and ran a search for psychiatrists in the Bondville area. Only one came up. *I guess he'll have to do.* He reached for his cell phone and thumbed in the number. The receptionist answered after three rings.

"Dr. Conway's office. How can I help you?" she answered in a chipper tone.

"Hi, I'd like to make an appointment with the doctor. I'm new in town, so I'll be a new patient," he murmured.

The receptionist, whose name turned out to be Carol, eagerly assisted him with establishing his first appointment. He was scheduled for 1:00 that day, due to a last-minute cancellation.

After he hung up with Carol, Rhett looked around the room. He still had so much to do and wanted to get something done before his appointment. He considered unpacking some more items, but then he decided that would make more sense after he'd fixed the cabinets. So, with tools in hand, he started on the ones in the kitchen. While working, he listened to one of the few channels he could get on the radio. After a couple of songs, the DJ started in with the news broadcast. He began talking about a morning pile-up on I-95 and then switched to a story about a local murder. Static began to drown out the story, though, so Rhett didn't get to hear the details.

By the time he was finished with most of the kitchen cabinets, it was time to clean up for his appointment with Dr. Conway. He went upstairs, whistling "California Girls" along the way. He abruptly stopped in the doorway to his bedroom and peered inside. He had the keen sense that something was different, but he couldn't figure out what it was. Shaking it off, he got clean clothes and headed to the bathroom for a shower. He hadn't noticed the sunlight glinting off the change jar, which was sitting on top of his dresser.

CHAPTER FIFTEEN

Rhett sat in the stuffy waiting room at Dr. Conway's office and thought about what he would say once he got in there. Obviously, he would talk about Laura, which would be the first time he ever talked about her with someone who wasn't family. Aside from her, though, he really didn't know how to begin. He didn't know what to say about the strange happenings around his home.

He had around twenty more minutes to kill before his appointment, so he picked up the daily newspaper lying on the side table, and a strange sense of déjà vu overcame him. He smoothed it out and read the front-page headline. "Local woman found shot in her office."

"Excuse me, Mr. Shaw, but I need you to fill out new patient paperwork," Carol suddenly called out from her seat behind the glass partition.

Rhett set the newspaper back down on the table and rose to fetch the clipboard containing several pages of health history forms to fill out. The first page was the standard personal information page. He hesitated at the address part, though. He knew it was Jones Drive, but he had to think hard about the house number, even though it was the only house. He squinted his eyes and tried to mentally picture the front of the house. The numbers were falling off the siding, but they were still visible because they were etched in the coat of dirt surrounding them.

"One hundred," he reminded himself, tapping the tip of the pen on the clipboard.

"I'm sorry?" Carol chirped from her desk. "Did you say something?"

Rhett felt his cheeks burn. The last place you want to get caught talking to yourself is at a psychiatrist's office.

"No," he mumbled.

Carol's phone buzzed then, and she quietly announced, "Mr. Shaw, the doctor will see you now. Go through the door to the second room on the left, please."

Rhett took a deep breath and walked to Dr. Conway's office, which looked more like a small library. Multiple shelves held books, and leather armchairs were placed neatly around the room.

The middle-aged doctor stood up and walked around his desk with his hand out. "It's nice to meet you, Mr. Shaw. I'm Dr. Conway."

"Hello," Rhett replied while firmly shaking the man's hand.

"Please choose a seat where you'll feel the most comfortable," Dr. Conway told him and gestured to the furniture.

Rhett couldn't help but wonder if choosing one particular chair over another was some kind of test. He plopped down in the closest one, and Dr. Conway sat in another, after facing it toward Rhett.

"I've only seen a therapist once," Rhett felt compelled to explain, "so, I might be a little nervous."

"It's okay, Mr. Shaw. I want you to feel at ease with me and just speak to me like you would a friend."

Rhett chuckled softly. "That might be a problem. I haven't been around any friends since—

" his voice trailed off on a sigh, and he looked away from the doctor's probing stare.

"Since what? What happened in your life to change that?" the doctor probed.

"Since my wife passed away," Rhett mumbled.

"I see, and how long ago was that?"

Rhett already felt the tears stinging his eyes. "Three years ago," he choked out.

The doctor wrote something down in his notebook. "Would you like to tell me about it? Was she ill? Was there an accident?"

Rhett wiped the pooled moisture away with the back of his hand. "She died from a brain aneurysm," he said with a shaky voice. He was fighting back the tears as much as he could; although, he doubted he was the first man to cry in the doctor's office.

Dr. Conway wrote more in his notebook and commented, "I think it's harder when death is sudden like that. I imagine she was close in age to you, so it's not something you'd be expected to prepare for. It must have been quite a shock."

With a light chuckle, Rhett said, "Well, we did live in Brooklyn, so we were always worried about crime. Otherwise, we were perfectly healthy, so yes, it came as a shock."

The doctor looked up with his pen poised. "So, you are from Brooklyn then. Did you move here right after?"

Rhett punctuated his answer with a shake of his head. "No, I just moved here a few days ago."

"Was it just time for a change in scenery, or did a job bring you here?"

Rhett nodded this time. "It was time for a change. I needed to get away from the noise, the crowds"—his voice got softer, and he looked away—"the memories."

"Is it helping yet? Do you feel any better here?" Dr. Conway queried while making more notes.

Rhett wore a tense smile. "Actually, that's kind of the real reason I'm here. Some weird things have been happening to me since I moved here."

The doctor's brow went up. "Like what?"

Rhett went on to explain about the strange noises, the locked door, the reflection in the mirror, and even the bloody handprint while the doctor took vigorous notes. He finished by saying, "So, I feel like I'm going crazy."

The doctor looked up with a serious expression. "I don't like to use the term 'crazy.' What I think is that you've been under emotional duress for three years now, and you expected a quick fix with your move. It was going to be a clean slate for you. However, going away doesn't mean your problems will go away. We can't escape our emotional baggage."

Rhett nodded to show that he was listening.

"Moving can be exciting, but it can also cause anxiety. I think in your case, by leaving what was familiar, you've heightened your anxiety," Dr. Conway explained.

Rhett mulled over the doctor's words. "That may be true, but part of me thinks it's the house I moved into. There's just something about it. I'm refurbishing the entire place, and when I work on it, it's like something is pulling me into the work. It's like the house *needs* me to work on it."

Dr. Conway peered at him through slatted eyes. "Well, I think you are displacing your love for your wife to the house. You need it to need you like she may have needed you, especially at the end of her life when there wasn't anything you could do to help her." He got up and crossed the room to his desk. A minute later, he handed a prescription to Rhett. "This is a mild tranquilizer to help you relax. Take it at bedtime first because it may make you drowsy. If you have any bothersome side effects, give me a call, and I'll switch you to something else. I'd like to see you again in a month, so make an appointment with Carol on your way out."

Rhett looked at the paper he held and then stood while holding his hand out. "Thanks, doc. I'll see you in one month."

He booked his appointment before leaving and filled the prescription at the pharmacy on the first floor. He knew he should stop off at the hardware store for the lightbulbs and other things he still needed, but he just wanted to go home. Creepy or not, he wanted to see his house.

CHAPTER SIXTEEN

It was 2:30 when Rhett returned home, so he had plenty of daylight yet to keep working on the house. The question was, though, on what? He thought about finishing the kitchen cabinets but decided to hold off on them. He glanced over his shoulder toward the front porch and considered finishing the railing. But that idea didn't appeal to him either. He looked around the living room area and settled on working on the flooring.

He began by checking the sub-floor for squeaks, and when he found some, he screwed drywall screws into the sub-floor and joist. He was in the middle of rolling out and fastening the asphalt-laminated kraft paper when his cell phone rang. It was Dave calling again.

"Hey, Dave," he answered with a sigh. "What's up?"

"I'm calling to see if you'll be sending any more chapters to me today," the editor pushed.

"Dave, you're killing me. I'm remodeling my new place, and that's a shit ton of work. I'll write more today, but probably not until after dark."

Now Dave was the one who sighed. "Rhett, I still want to get the book in the hands of buyers next spring. You haven't been pounding this one out like you did the others, and that concerns me. I need time for edits, then rewrites, and then the publisher will need their time with it too."

"Dave," Rhett began with an exasperated tone, "you aren't telling me anything I don't already know. But this is a new genre for me, so I have to get my sea legs yet. Once I get into character, I'm sure I'll make real progress. Right now, however, I'm trying to put in flooring, so I need to get off the phone. I'm sure I'll have something for you later today."

"I hope so. We'll talk again soon." Dave disconnected the line.

Rhett finished attaching the kraft paper, removed the shoe molding, and began laying the new floor. He only stopped to eat dinner. It was already 8:00 when he finished putting the new boards down, and his knees were screaming at him. He went through a packed box of toiletries and found his muscle rub. Then after rubbing a copious amount on each knee, he sat down at his laptop and opened the Word document containing his book.

He reviewed the last part he'd added and decided to start back up with detective Rodney Small.

GET
OUT

Rodney quickly walked out of the captain's office with his tail tucked between his legs. He didn't need the ass chewing on top of his already difficult day.

First, his alarm clock had failed to go off, then he'd spilled hot coffee on himself during the rush hour commute to the office, where the captain had immediately greeted him with an angry "come see me" hand gesture.

He was yelled at for twenty minutes about his lack of progress on the recent string of homicides he was investigating. He had seven murders already with no suspects. He wasn't even sure that the same man was responsible for each one—he just had a feeling it was serial. Without any leads to go on, he felt like he was standing around with his thumb up his ass, and that's what the captain accused him of. Whoever the killer was, he was taking precautions not to leave prints or DNA.

Rodney couldn't help but wonder about the lack of sexual assault. The murdered Latina had been tied up, yet the perp didn't rape her. The title loan office was locked with just one woman, but again, there wasn't an assault. Rodney wondered if the killer struggled with impotence. That could explain the violent nature in which the Latina had been killed.

"Why switch from a knife to a gun? Maybe I'm after more than one perp, or possibly, I'm after a woman. Great," Rodney thought aloud.

The Latina was missing a chunk of hair, which could point to a woman as the doer. Maybe the killer felt compulsive to disfigure the victim. Then again, it was common for serial killers to take trinkets, so they could relive the crime whenever they wanted to, but as far as he knew, nothing was missing from the other crime scenes. That also pointed to the possibility of more than one perp.

Rodney scratched his head and plopped down at his desk to go through the files—again. He looked at the crime scene photos and the few statements they had taken. No one had seen or heard anything. *So they said.*

He jotted down notes about his killer. He was probably working a menial job, if he was working at all, and he was narcissistic. He most likely felt that society owed him for something since theft was a common denominator in each crime. *Well, shit. I just described a quarter of the city's population.* No matter how hard he tried, he couldn't get into the killer's head. He couldn't figure out what the next move would be.

He reached into his desk drawer and pulled out a packet of papers to look over again. It was an application form for early retirement. He thumbed through them once and then shoved them back inside his desk. He couldn't just walk away leaving this case open.

GET
OUT

Rhett considered starting the next chapter, starring Jack, when his phone rang again. He scowled, thinking it was Dave, but the display said it was an unknown number.

"Hello?" he answered, but there was only silence. "Hello?" he asked again, but with mounting aggravation in his voice. *It's probably a telemarketer.* Silence still greeted him, and he was about to hang up when he suddenly heard breathing on the other end. "Hello, who is this?"

A sinister chuckle came across the line, followed by thumping and snarling sounds. Then a raspy voice said, "Hello? Hello?" before turning into evil laughter again.

Rhett quickly ended the prank call. Dismissing it, he turned back to his laptop and poised his fingers to type. Before he could press the keys, though, something typed itself onto the screen.

It read "Hello? Hello?"

CHAPTER SEVENTEEN

Rhett stared at the screen and then at his trembling hands. The words on the page kept him frozen in his seat, but his brain screamed at him to run. He gulped hard and noticed how dry his mouth had become. He was too afraid to even blink. A chill wracked through his body, causing his teeth to chatter. There was no explanation for what he was seeing.

"Unless someone hacked my laptop," he told himself.

The possibility, as frightening as it would be, comforted him enough to start moving again. The only other explanation would be something supernatural, and he might go there in his books, but he didn't want to go there in reality. He took a deep cleansing breath and deleted the words. Then he dug out the bottle of pills the doctor had prescribed and took the recommended dose with a sip of soda. It was almost time for bed anyway. He went into the kitchen and threw away the empty soda can into the loose trash bag he had sitting on the floor. Tomorrow, he'd need to get his trash cans.

He went back to his desk and thought about how to pick up where he'd left off in the story, but then he decided to close the document and send the recent chapter to Dave. It wasn't much, but it would have to do. He didn't have the strength to produce any more material that night. He chose to watch some sitcoms instead, so he opened Netflix. He scrolled through the list and settled on

Friends—it had been one of Laura's favorite shows, and he needed to feel closer to her right then. He picked up where he'd last watched it, and that was at the point when Ross and Rachel were having a baby. It made him think, again, about not having had any kids with Laura. They'd been together for six years when she died, and they'd talked about children on occasion but never attempted to conceive. They finally came to an agreement that they'd start looking for a home in the country and then would try for a child after moving. That decision was made one month before she died.

He looked around the empty living room and tried to picture a toddler sitting on the sofa next to him. He wondered if the child would've been blessed with Laura's golden blonde hair and sparkling blue eyes. He knew she would've made a terrific mother.

A wide yawn escaped him as drowsiness set in, so he turned off the computer and headed up the steps. When he got to the top, he noticed a glowing light underneath the door to the small bedroom. Trembling, he quickly opened it, not knowing what to expect, but the room was dark. He flipped the light on and looked around the empty room. Everything looked the same until he noticed something in the corner. He walked over and picked it up. It was a child's stuffed bear—and it hadn't been there before. He threw the bear back to the floor and rubbed his tired eyes. He had to be imagining things. He just missed seeing the bear before. There wasn't any other logical explanation. *Right?*

He shut the bedroom door again and dragged himself to bed. He left the closet light on, though, and his arm hairs remained upright.

CHAPTER EIGHTEEN

Rhett woke up shivering under the blanket. It was late spring, so it shouldn't be this cold, yet the chill in the air made his bones ache. He climbed out of bed, seeing his breath when he exhaled, and grabbed a sweatshirt and jeans out of his dresser. He quickly threw them on and went downstairs to check the thermostat. It read 65 degrees—he'd had it set at 72. He dialed it back up and then went over to his desk to add it to a list of things he needed to purchase. He ticked them off one by one. He would get a new thermostat, trash cans, light bulbs, a floor sander, and varnish. He also needed more groceries.

He turned on his laptop and went directly to his email. He had a message from Jeremy, who wanted to know where he'd ended up moving to and how he was doing. Rhett typed a short response and sent it off. He also had a message from Dave regarding the most recent chapter. He commented favorably about the content, but again complained that he'd expected more than just the one short chapter. Rhett rolled his gray eyes and drummed his fingers on the desk. He was going to need to step up his game and produce a considerable amount of material. He didn't want to have to find a new editor.

As he tried to get into the story, though, he found he couldn't concentrate. He looked at the floor beneath his bare feet, and a strong urge to complete it overcame him. He ran up the stairs, brushed his teeth, combed his hair, and put on socks and work boots. He was out the front door five minutes later, skipping his morning coffee.

He drove to the hardware store first. He had forgotten about tiles for the bathroom and kitchen until he saw them on display. He chose a light tan pattern for the kitchen, so it would match the light oak flooring in the living room. He went with a light blue pattern for the bathroom. He walked through the aisles and looked for the items on his list but checked everything else out, too, just in case there were more things he'd forgotten. He grabbed shelf liner for the cabinets and hall closet, light bulbs, varnish, and a new thermostat. Then he grabbed the trash cans he needed. He rolled the heavy shopping cart up to the service counter and patiently waited in line for his turn.

"How may I help you?" the young female clerk greeted him.

"Hi, I need a sander I can rent for a few days. Do I do that with you?"

She smiled broadly. "Yes, but our only one is checked out right now. Let me look to see when it's due back." She typed several keys and then scrolled her finger down the screen. "Ah, here it is. It shows that it's due back tomorrow morning. So, you can rent it then by filling out some paperwork now. That way, we can hold it for you," she explained in a chipper voice.

"Oh." He clapped his hands together and rubbed his calloused palms. He didn't want to wait until tomorrow, but he also didn't want to run around town hoping to find another hardware store. "Okay, I guess I'll just do that then."

"Great! Here's the paper for you to fill out, and then I'll need a ten percent deposit on the first day's rental fee."

"Sure," Rhett mumbled while taking the pen and form she was holding out to him. He stepped to the side so she could help the next person in line.

The form collected personal information about him and also his credit card information. It only took a couple of minutes to fill it out and get back in line. He handed her the pen and paper, which she then looked over.

"Okay, let me just get you added to our customer database. Is this the card you want to pay with, or would you like to apply for one of our store cards?"

Rhett shook his head. "No, I'll just use the one I listed."

Her face fell. "Are you sure? You can save twenty percent on the rental and all the stuff in your cart by opening an account with us today."

"I understand, Jennifer, but I'm going to stick with the card I already have," he replied, and his tone was more clipped than he wished for it to be. "But thanks anyway," he added apologetically.

"Sure, that's fine. I have everything entered, and the sander is reserved for tomorrow. You can pick it up any time after 9:00 a.m."

"Thank you," he replied and left the desk to find an available cashier.

After the Jeep was loaded, he made his way to the grocery store. IGA was especially busy this time, so navigating the crowded aisles with his cart was a chore. Not liking big crowds anymore, Rhett avoided eye contact as much as possible. He felt that people could read on his face that he was a widower and would feel sorry for him. He didn't want that.

Someone bumped into his cart with theirs. "Oh, hi!" a woman exclaimed, so he looked up. It was the lost woman from the other day. *What is her name? Bridget?*

"Hi. It's Bridget, right?" he asked just to be sure.

"Hi, Rhett. You have a good memory. How are the repairs on your house coming along?"

He ran his hand through his hair and sighed. "Slowly but surely," he said with a slight smile. "I'm ready to buff and stain the living room floor anyway, and I just need to finish the railing on the front porch so it'll be ready for painting."

"Wow, look at you. You're handy to have around, huh?" She looked up at him with admiration and fluttered her lashes.

"I guess so," he answered with modesty.

Bridget looked at his left hand, and her eyes widened. "I didn't notice your wedding ring the other day. I thought you said you lived alone." She raised her brow at him.

Rhett looked down at his hand with just as much surprise. He didn't normally wear his ring, and he didn't remember slipping it on either. True, he'd worn it for a long time after Laura died, but then he'd put it away in a box with his good watch, which was now stuffed in the top dresser drawer. Of course, he'd taken the new medicine last night and was drowsy when he went to bed, so maybe without thinking, he'd slipped it on.

"I am. I mean, I do live alone. I'm a widower," he mumbled.

"Oh, I'm so sorry," she replied softly. "It's sweet that you still wear your ring." She nodded toward his hand.

"I guess so," he said and shrugged. Then, to change the topic, he looked at the items in her cart and asked, "Are you cooking dinner for your sister again?"

Her lips turned up, flashing her dimples. "No. She has plans, so it's just me tonight." She looked at the TV dinners stacked neatly in his shopping cart. "It looks like it's just you tonight, too."

Rhett smiled. "It's just me every night." He saw the questioning look in her eyes, so he elaborated. "I mean, I haven't dated since my wife passed away three years ago."

She pursed her lips, and her eyes went wide again. "That's a long time to be alone. You know, I have more food here than I can eat by myself, so why don't I bring it over and cook for you?" She immediately saw the hesitation in his eyes, so she added, "We can talk about your first book. I started reading it the other night."

"Really? That's cool. Um, I guess if you want to discuss the book, that'd be okay. My house is still a huge mess, but you're welcome to come over." He saw a look of pleasure play across her face, so he felt the need to add, "I'm not ready for dating, but a friend dropping by wouldn't hurt."

She briefly looked disappointed, but she forced a smile and told him, "Okay. Well, how about 6:00? Will that be a good time? You can work on the house while I cook."

Rhett smiled warmly at her. "Sure. That sounds nice. I need to finish shopping and get home, but I'll see you later today," he quickly replied before he could change his mind.

"Okay, bye," she said, and her green eyes sparkled.

As she walked off toward the checkout lines, Rhett couldn't help but wonder if he was making a big mistake. He hadn't been alone with any woman other than Laura in over nine years. *This isn't a date, though.* He reminded himself of what he'd told Bridget. Still, he did like watching the sway of her hips as she walked away from him.

He tore his eyes away from her and went back to his shopping. He grabbed more bread, some fruit, soup, beer, and another case of soda before going to the checkout line. Then he drove straight home.

A weird feeling overcame him as he parked in his driveway. He felt like the house was happy to see him.

CHAPTER NINETEEN

Rhett was working on the staircase when there was a soft knock on the front door. He looked down at his watch and saw that it was ten minutes until 6:00. He'd been working so diligently on the steps that time had slipped away from him. He hadn't even showered. *I guess that's one way to prove it's not a date.* He pulled a handkerchief out of his pocket and mopped at his sweaty face.

He saw her through the glass window on the door, which he quickly swung open. Her arms were full of grocery bags.

"Hi, Bridget," he said and stepped aside.

"Hi. I hope it's okay that I'm a few minutes early. I didn't know what traffic would be like at this time of day," she hollered over his blaring radio.

"Sure, it's fine. I'm still dirty, though, and I apologize for that," he replied, turning the volume down. "I lost track of time."

"Oh, no worries. Um...Can I go into the kitchen and get started? You'll have to show me where your pots and pans are, but then I'll take it from there."

Rhett took the bags from her and led the way into the kitchen. He showed her the cabinet holding his skillets and pots. He pulled a cookie sheet out from the stove drawer because he saw that she'd bought garlic toast too.

"Spatulas, ladles, and such are in this drawer"—he pointed—"and there are knives in that one."

"Okay. Well, that should be all I need, so you can do your thing, and I'll be in here doing mine," she told him with a dimpled smile.

He grinned back and replied, "That sounds like a plan. Holler if you need me." He went back to his work on the staircase and left the meal preparation to her.

It was about twenty minutes later when the delicious aroma of lasagna wafted to him and made his mouth water. He didn't know what she was making next, but there was a loud clash of pots followed by an expletive from her.

"Is everything okay?" he called out to her.

"Yeah. I'm sorry about the noise and my potty mouth," she hollered back.

He shook his head with an amused grin and turned his focus back to the step he was working on. After hammering the board firmly in place, he used sanding paper to smooth it out. It was, thankfully, the last step to replace. He sat on the landing, looked down the length of the staircase, and wondered if he should cover them with carpeting. He decided that it would only look good if he put a large area rug in the living room that matched. He tried to tap into Laura's sense of style. She would've insisted on it, he was sure, so he made a mental note to look at the carpeting and rugs the next time he was in the hardware store.

He jogged down the stairs and to the kitchen to check on Bridget. "It smells good in here," he announced.

"Well, just give me about fifteen more minutes, and I'll have it on the table," she informed him. "I hope you're hungry."

He rubbed his stomach. "Famished. I'm going to hop into the shower while you finish up."

"Sounds good." She bobbed her head while opening the oven to check on the dish.

He spun on his heel and headed upstairs where he took a five-minute shower. When he climbed out of the stall into the steamy room, he noticed something odd about the bathroom mirror. "Help" was written in the condensation.

CHAPTER TWENTY

Rhett felt self-conscious and angry as he descended the stairs. He couldn't believe she came into the bathroom while he was showering to write "help" on the mirror. She probably thought it was funny, but he felt like his privacy was violated. The shower curtain was transparent with small diamond shapes on it, so she would've seen everything. *Why didn't I see her then?*

He walked into the kitchen to find her setting the meal out on the new table, which he'd not even used yet. He hadn't even peeled the protective plastic off the seat cushions yet, which was unfortunate because it made an unpleasant sound when he sat down.

"Plastic," he mumbled with a smile because he saw a smirk on her face. He swallowed back the anger he'd been feeling because he just wanted to forget about the whole thing. He was never good at confrontation.

"Do you like wine? I always drink wine with Italian cuisine, so I brought a bottle." She sat down the salad she was carrying and reached into the last shopping bag to produce a bottle of Merlot.

"Sure, I love it. Let me get the glasses down," he offered because she wasn't tall enough to reach the shelf holding his wine glasses. He grabbed the first two he saw, but then he quickly put them back—they were the glasses from his wedding reception. He pushed them to the back of the cabinet and grabbed two generic ones.

"Which kind of dressing do you want for your salad? I brought Italian, Ranch, Cesar, and French."

"Wow. You thought of everything, didn't you? Actually, I prefer Thousand Island, though," he told her with a playful grin.

Her smile turned down. "Really? I'm sorry. I thought I grabbed enough kinds."

Rhett chuckled. "I'm just kidding. I like them all, but Italian goes with lasagna, so I'll have that tonight." He put plates and silverware on the table next to the wine glasses.

Bridget breathed a sigh of relief. "Whew. You had me there." She pulled the sheet of garlic toast out of the oven and put it on the back burner before turning the stove off. "How many slices would you like?"

"Just one for now, please," he answered.

She got their plates and put one piece of toast on each while he poured the wine. Then she joined him at the table.

"Are you going back home soon?" he asked in between bites.

"Yes, I leave the day after tomorrow. It was a nice spring break, though. I enjoyed seeing my sister and meeting a famous author."

Rhett felt himself blush. "You flatter me. I'd hardly call myself famous."

She flicked her wrist at him. "You're too modest. I saw your hundreds of reviews, and I'm enjoying book one."

"That's awesome," he said with a smile. "Do you read a lot of paranormal romances?"

"I've read a few, but they weren't as good as *Wolfsbane*," she told him with a wink. "Are you working on book three now?"

He looked up from his plate and met her gaze. "No, I'm writing a crime story now. It's a challenge to switch genres, but I like it so far."

"Oh, cool. Tell me about it."

Rhett explained the plot of his book, and then they discussed *Wolfsbane* in detail while they finished their meal.

"That was amazing," he said while patting his stomach. "Thank you for cooking."

She smiled while wrapping up the leftovers. "You're welcome, and I'm glad you liked it. My sister always complains that I use too much garlic."

"Nope. It was excellent. Would you like another glass of wine? We could sit on the front porch and enjoy the sunset."

"Yes, please."

They took their glasses out to the porch and sat on the swing. It made a metallic whining sound as it slowly swung back and forth. She'd sat a little closer to him than what he was comfortable with, but he didn't want to seem rude by inching away. He noticed her perfume for the first time and found that he liked it.

"Can I ask you something?" she suddenly asked.

"Sure. Go ahead."

She turned her body to face him. "Why are you spending all of your time and money fixing this house up? I'm sure there are plenty of houses around that aren't so run-down."

"I don't know. I guess it called out to me. It needs some TLC is all, and I like working with my hands." He kept his words polite, but his skin prickled with irritation.

"Humph. It needs a major overhaul," she sniped, and her face pinched in a scowl.

Before he could defend his house, and he was prepared to do so, there was a loud popping sound, and the swing crashed to the ground on her side. He swallowed the laughter that was bubbling up.

"Ouch! Shit, I'm bleeding," she exclaimed, and he looked to see her broken glass buried in her palm.

"Let's get you inside. I have a first-aid kit," Rhett said and helped her up from the ground, biting back a smug smile.

He led her to the kitchen and retrieved the kit. Using a pair of tweezers, he carefully removed the chunks of glass from her hand. Then he washed the wound with hydrogen peroxide and wrapped it up with gauze and bandages.

"You're pretty good at that. Are you sure you weren't in medicine before?" she asked, still wincing from the pain.

He gave her a slight smile. "I'm sorry about the swing. I should've replaced the chains on it before using it. And as for the bandages, I needed them a lot when I worked construction. I paid attention to what Laura was doing when she fixed me up. She was a nurse." His voice trailed off when he mentioned his wife.

"I can see that you really miss her. It's on your face and in your voice," she observed. "May I ask, how long ago was her passing? I know you told me, but I forgot what you said."

His face grew tight with pain, and he turned away from her. Instead of answering with a humiliating, quivering voice, he held up three fingers.

"Oh, that's right. Your grief is still fresh then," she mumbled in a consoling tone.

Rhett nodded, still turned away from her. He didn't want her to see his tears. He found his voice, though. "I'd like to get back to work on the house. Would you mind if I called it a night?"

"Um, sure. I understand. I'm glad you enjoyed dinner. I go back home in two days, so maybe I'll call on you when I come through the area again. I'll follow your fan page, too, so I can keep up with your writing."

He turned to face her. "Thank you. I'd appreciate that. I'll walk you out, and again, I'm sorry about the swing."

She laughed lightly and rose from the kitchen chair. "I think it was a reminder to stick to my diet. I've been eating high off the hog since vacation started."

Rhett automatically looked down at her waistline. "You look great. You don't need to diet."

She waved off the compliment. "Thank you, but I do. My jeans are getting tighter." She laughed again, and Rhett couldn't deny that he liked the sound of it.

It's been such a long time since I've heard a woman's laughter.

Without warning, she stood on her tiptoes and planted a kiss on his cheek. "It was good to spend time with you, Rhett. I wish you'd put yourself back on the market, but I understand how difficult it must be for you."

He looked down at his shoes and slowly shook his head. "I can't. I just can't. I don't know that I'll ever be able to date again. Laura was my entire world for six years."

Bridget spoke softly. "I understand, but what would she want for you? Think about that before you shut yourself off permanently from the world."

Rhett forced a tight smile. "I will," he lied. He glanced down the drive to the next street. He felt like they were being watched, but he didn't see anyone. He quickly looked over his shoulder at the house. Out of the corner of his eye, he thought he saw movement in his bedroom window.

"Um, I need to get to work on my repairs. Take care," he mumbled without looking back at the woman. Instead, he kept his eyes focused on the empty window. He'd been sure *something* was there, and he could still feel its presence.

CHAPTER TWENTY-ONE

Rhett ran through the upstairs area, then downstairs, and finally the basement. Nothing. His eyes were playing tricks on him again. He went into the bathroom and popped his anxiety medication. It was only 8:00, but maybe he just needed to get more sleep. Maybe tonight, he wouldn't have nightmares about his sweet Laura.

He trotted back down the steps and picked up his hammer from where he'd left it. He looked around the room and at the tool, which he then put back down. He needed to write, especially before the medication made him too drowsy to do so. He turned his laptop on and checked his email first, surprised there wasn't anything from Dave. He was sure, though, that there would be something from him tomorrow if he didn't crank out at least one more chapter before then.

He sighed and ran both hands through his hair as he tried to pick up where he'd left off. He typed a few lines, but then deleted them. He couldn't clear his mind enough to think. He knew he wasn't supposed to mix alcohol with the new medication, but he finished off his glass of wine anyway. Maybe it would spark his creativity. He rubbed his eyes and stared at the blinking cursor, demanding that he write something. He closed his eyes and concentrated, trying to get into Jack's mindset. He would feel powerful and confident after pulling off his latest crime. He'd probably clip newspaper articles on the murders, so he could keep reliving the experience. He would want to see how the media glorified him and his work. Rhett poised his fingers and began to type.

GET
OUT

Jack woke up late on Sunday, feeling refreshed. He smiled as he recalled his eventful Saturday. He licked his lips as he recalled how the fear had clouded the woman's face. Her trembling had only added to his excitement. He closed his eyes and recalled the tortured look on her face as her soul had left her body. She'd stared at him while taking her last breath, and it exhilarated him. If only he could've made it last longer.

He climbed out of bed, stepping on a bug, and headed to the shower. He had to wait until the dirty water ran clear before he hopped in. A couple of spiders scurried around the shower stall and made him cringe. He had to get out of this dump, and he knew just what to do. When he was finished dressing, he headed to the parking lot.

"Bye. I won't be home tonight," he said quietly to himself while throwing a glance over his shoulder at the run-down roach motel.

He drove through nicer areas of town until he found his mark. An elderly woman was checking her mail, and she was alone. He pulled up and called out to her. "Excuse me, but I'm lost. Do you think you could point me in the direction of Lincoln Park?" He made sure to sound kind, so she would trust him.

"Well, I'm not sure that I know where that is either," she replied in a gravelly voice, pinpointing her as a heavy smoker. "You could come inside, though, and talk to my husband. He always does the driving."

"That'd be great," Jack replied with a warm smile and parked his beater in her driveway. He slowly climbed out with his gun tucked away in the back of his waistband and followed the wobbling woman inside.

An elderly man's voice rang out, "It took you long enough. Where's my lunch?"

She began explaining, "This young ma—" she broke off, having heard the click of the lock on the front door behind her. She turned around as quickly as she could, which was slow, and her eyes widened with terror when she saw the gun aimed at her.

"What?" the old man called out.

"I-I-I," she sputtered, too terrified to scream, and backed up toward the entrance to the living room.

Her husband tried to climb out of his chair when she rounded the corner—until he saw what was happening—then he fell back. "What the hell do you want?" he asked in the toughest voice he could muster, but Jack saw his knees knocking together as his body shook uncontrollably.

Jack chuckled to himself and looked around the nice living room. "Just your house, old man." He pressed the gun into the woman's back and fired. The bullet passed through her frail body and into her husband, who slumped over while she fell to the ground. *Two old birds with one stone.*

Jack dragged the bodies to the basement in garbage bags. He put them in the farthest corner and covered them up with their laundry to conceal the odor as they began to decompose. He intended to stay in the house for a couple of days, and he didn't want to smell the rot. Then he pulled his car into their garage and switched his license plates for the ones on their Lincoln Town Car. The vehicle had tinted windows, which would help conceal his identity. *Talk about an upgrade.* Luckily, no one was outside to observe what he was doing.

He went through the house and the old woman's jewelry box, looking for anything he could sell. She had a lot of gold necklaces, rings, and bracelets he could liquidate and a fur coat he could pawn. He went through the mail she'd dropped and found their Social Security checks and smiled. He knew of a check cashing place that never asked questions and never asked for ID.

He looked behind all the paintings and furniture, looking for a wall safe, but he didn't find any. He looked into the old woman's purse and saw the tidy sum they held in their checking account. The bank they used had three branches in town, so if he went to the one that was farthest away, he could probably cash a check. He wrote the check out to cash, signed the old man's name, and headed to the bank after locking the house up tight.

"After all, criminals could be lurking around," he mused to himself.

GET
OUT

Rhett went back over the chapter with a satisfied smile but heavy eyelids. After he proofread it, he sent it off to Dave and trudged upstairs to bed. He quickly fell asleep and began to dream. He didn't dream about Laura, though. Instead, he dreamed about Bridget. He dreamed that she was trapped inside his house, and it was on fire. He tried to get inside to help her, but the door was stuck. He broke in the closest window, but the oxygen only made the flames leap higher, causing a bigger barrier for him. He looked up at the flaming house and saw her screaming face in the window. He also saw someone standing behind her as the flames licked her flesh.

CHAPTER TWENTY-TWO

Rhett woke up in a cold sweat. He saw a sliver of light coming in through the window and looked at his clock. It was a few minutes past 6:00, and there was no way he would fall back to sleep after that dream, so he got up. He dressed and used the bathroom before going straight to the kitchen to start a pot of industrial-strength coffee. While it brewed, he went to his desk and powered on his laptop. He was surprised to see that he still didn't have an email from Dave, but he was also relieved. He didn't want to be nagged anymore, especially not this morning—something had him in a grouchy mood.

Rhett filled the biggest mug he had to the rim and plopped down in front of his book. He reread over his previous chapter and considered where to go next, but his head began to pound, so he closed the document. He stepped out onto the front porch and sat on the top step since the swing was broken. He recalled the gaping wound in her palm from the glass. There had been so much blood. It made him sick to his stomach to think about it now. He glanced in the swing's direction to see how much blood he would have to clean up and became nauseous from the sight of it.

His cell phone beeped and pulled his attention away from the mess. His battery was warning him that it was only at ten percent, so he got up to go inside and plug it in. He noticed that it was 6:30 already, and he couldn't pick the floor sander up until 9:00, so that allowed enough time for more repairs.

He studied the vinyl flooring in the kitchen to see where its weakest spots were. Then using pliers and a scraper tool, he started ripping it up from the northeast corner. He made progress foot by foot. Luckily, the previous decorators hadn't used a stronger adhesive when they laid the vinyl. Unfortunately, though, moisture had collected in some areas, and mold was growing. He donned a mask and rubber gloves before scrubbing at the mold with bleach. When he was finished, it was 8:30 and time to head to the hardware store.

GET
OUT

A different clerk was running the service desk this time. The cashier had helped Rhett a couple of times before, though, and he recognized him today.

"You're back," he greeted Rhett. "Still making repairs, huh?"

Rhett smiled back at the clerk. "You know it. There's a lot to do yet. I'm here to rent the sander. I filled out my paperwork for it yesterday."

The man started flipping through the rental contracts. "Last name's Shaw, right?"

"Yes. You have a good memory."

The man looked up with a quirky smile. "Well, you're one of our best customers."

Rhett laughed at the obvious compliment. "I bet you say that to everyone."

The clerk pulled one of the contracts from the file folder. "Here it is. You have it rented until tomorrow. Will that give you enough time? I can always put in more days if you think you'll need it longer."

Rhett rubbed his chin. "You know, that's not a bad idea. Let me keep it for two more days if I can."

"Sure! That's no problem. I just need to amend the paperwork, so give me a minute." He started typing up the new contract on the computer, but then he stopped and looked up at Rhett with a raised brow. "This says your address is 100 Jones Drive. The cashier must've typed that in wrong. What is it please?"

Now, Rhett was the one who looked confused. "No, that's right. She typed it correctly. I mean the letters are falling off the house, but I'm sure that it's 100, and it's the only house on the drive anyway," he said with a shrug.

"*Jones* Drive, Bondville?"

Rhett's brows came together, and his jaw clenched until it hurt. Forcing himself to remain calm, he replied, "Yes, Jones Drive in Bondville. Why? What's the problem here?"

The man looked at the computer, back at Rhett, and then back at the computer. His hands were trembling as much as his voice was when he told Rhett, "You couldn't possibly live on Jones Drive in Bondville."

"Why the hell not?" His voice boomed through the store, causing several heads to turn in their direction.

The clerk drew quick breaths and stared at the monitor, avoiding Rhett's glare at all cost.

Hesitantly, he answered, "Because the house on Jones Drive burned down six years ago, Mr. Shaw. It killed the entire family living there."

The world suddenly stood still. . .

CHAPTER TWENTY-THREE

Rhett drove as fast as he could to the library he'd seen in town. His stomach felt heavy whereas his head felt light, and his skin tingled uncomfortably all over as if a thousand ants marched across it. "The house on Jones Drive burned down six years ago." The clerk's words reverberated through his racing mind. The man had to be mistaken. Still, there had been strange noises, and he'd seen things—things that were never there. He could keep telling himself that he was just tired, but for how long? How long could he ignore his gut feeling that something wasn't right? That he wasn't always alone? His breathing grew shallow, and his clammy hands started to slip on the steering wheel.

He whipped the Jeep into the library parking lot and found a vacant space. Then he ran to the door, causing the library clerk to look up with a frown when it slammed shut behind him.

"Can I *help* you?" the middle-aged woman asked in a snooty voice.

He looked over his shoulder at the entrance and turned red. "Oh, sorry about the door. Where can I look up old newspaper articles?"

Still scowling at him, she pointed a bony finger to the nearby staircase. "Upstairs. They are stored on microfilm in the Archives Room. It's on the right."

Rhett slapped his hand on the counter, causing her to jump. "Thank you. I appreciate it."

He bolted up the steps with her disapproving stare burning a hole into his back.

The three machines were all available for use, so he sat at the first one. He quickly read the directions taped to the table and began his search. He searched for articles dating six years ago that had the words "Jones Drive." It seemed to take forever before the results populated, and there were several articles. They covered several Jones Drives throughout the state of Vermont, though, so he added "Bondville" to narrow the search. It gave him the hourglass symbol again while the machine processed the new keywords. He incessantly tapped his fingers on the table, and his leg knocked on the underside. The wait was aggravating, yet he was afraid of what he might find.

The machine finally announced that it was done with its search. Only a few articles popped up this time. The largest article was a front-page story about his house—well, Rob and Diane Jones's house. The headline read "Massive House Fire Kills Family of Four."

The room started to spin, and his throat grew dry and tight as he scrolled through the disturbing photos of the devastating fire. Ringing in his ears added to his stomach cramps, and he became nauseous. The photos showed the house scorched nearly to its foundation. Only part of the shell remained. There was, of course, a large photo of the family killed in the fire. Rob, 40, Diane, 37, Patrick, 10, and Sarah, 8, were asleep when the fire broke out around 1:00 a.m. on March 7, 2007. Neighbors on adjacent streets said that a loud explosion woke them up. It was too late when fire responders made it to the scene. It took firefighters forty minutes to put the blaze out, and the family was found inside. The Fire Chief had claimed that the fire wasn't suspicious and had likely originated in the kitchen, based on burn patterns, and had been caused by faulty wiring. The family simply didn't have the means to escape when the blaze traveled up the stairs.

Rhett shook as he read and re-read the articles. Tears traveled down his cheeks as he poured over the numerous statements about the Jones family from members of the community. They'd been regarded as having been quiet but polite. The children did well in school, and they never caused problems. The father worked as a plumber, and Diane Jones was a homemaker. They attended church regularly and helped with charitable events. To Rhett, they sounded like the Cleavers. It sounded like the life he could've had with Laura had they had the chance. He printed out the feature article and held it in his quivering hands. Staring at the page, though, still didn't make the story possible. Despite its run-down condition, there was no evidence of fire damage to his house. Maybe someone had already started the repairs. Maybe someone had lived there after the Joneses' tragedy.

It can't be the house in those photos. There's just no way. He repeated the declaration to himself a dozen times as he walked to his Jeep, paper still clutched in his clammy hand. However, there was nothing he could say to himself that would make him believe otherwise. The proof lay on the seat next to him, and he knew what he had to do—he had to leave town. *I won't live in a haunted house, even though it feels like it wants me there.*

CHAPTER TWENTY-FOUR

Rhett pulled into his driveway with a great deal of hesitation. The plan was to get in and get out. He would pack the necessities and not worry about the rest. He planned to leave with only the items he'd brought from New York. The new furniture would be a loss, but it wasn't like he couldn't afford to replace it. He left the sander sitting in the Jeep—he wouldn't need it now. He should've just left it at the store, but he'd gone into a daze after the news about the house. Everything after that had been mechanical until he'd reached the library and ran his search. Now, the sander was in the backseat mocking him. It was pointing out that his dream was over—he still didn't have a home to feel comfortable in. He felt like another part of his heart had just died.

He slowly opened the front door, feeling a chill as its loud creak filled the room. He stepped inside and immediately noticed that his laptop was turned on, and he was certain he'd not left it that way. He crept across the room and stared down at it. His book document was open, and the cursor flashed like a beacon of hope. It called out to him to write something witty and concrete that would summon the masses to local bookstores. People were attracted to murder, despite their fear, and he needed to give them what they wanted. He grabbed a beer from the refrigerator and sat down to write—completely engrossed in the ideas flooding his mind. There were no thoughts of leaving as he pounded the keys. Jack had work to do.

GET
OUT

Jack had successfully cashed the Social Security and personal checks and was now sitting comfortably on the sofa in his new house. At least, it would be his house for a couple of days—maybe even longer if no one came snooping. He turned on the TV. It was nice to have clear reception and tons of channels to surf through. He had lots of options to pick from. He noticed the time on the large screen and remembered that he was supposed to work the late shift for someone who'd filled in for him recently.

"Not gonna happen," he mused aloud.

He picked up the nearby telephone to call in sick but then thought better of it. His boss may have caller ID, and he didn't want to leave any trails to his whereabouts or connection to the elderly couple. He used his cell phone instead and told his boss that he had a bad case of the flu and wouldn't be in for a couple of days per his doctor's orders. He made sure to hack a few times and make his voice gravely. Whether he believed him or not, his boss excused him for two days.

"I will plan on seeing you Wednesday then," he said sternly.

Jack laughed to himself. He should just quit the shitty job and work crime full-time because it was paying a lot more. He had enough money now to move to a better apartment when he could no longer stay in the couple's house. He kicked his shoes off while settling on a re-run of *CSI Miami*. It was one of his favorite shows, and it served as a reminder to cover his tracks. So, he pulled out his pocketknife and picked a shoe up. He only had that pair and needed to alter the tread just in case he'd left footprints anywhere. He cut away at the rubber bottoms in a couple of spots and then did the same to the other. He had been careful to wear gloves every time, so, thankfully, he didn't need to alter his fingerprints. He wasn't into slicing and dicing himself up—just other people.

He briefly considered going out again that night, but staying in appealed to him too since he'd found such a nice place. He got up and went into the kitchen to see what they had to eat. He expected bland crackers and prunes, but he found steak, lobster, and a fresh apple pie. He located the correct dishes and started cooking. Luckily, his favorite foster mother had taught him how to cook when he was a kid. She said he'd make a woman happy one day if he knew his way around the kitchen, but he'd never come close to finding out if that was true or not. He scowled as he remembered his dreams of attending culinary school. It seemed like a lifetime had passed since he'd had those ambitions. Once he reached his sixteenth birthday, he no longer cared about higher education or having a career. He dropped out of high school, packed his backpack, and ran away from his abuser at the time.

Jack slammed his fist on the kitchen counter and instantly regretted it when shards of pain shot up his arm. It was the same arm that was covered in burn scars from countless cigarettes.

He turned off the stove, put the food back in the refrigerator, and headed out for the night. He'd get something to eat at a local bar, and then he'd find fresh prey. *Hell, I might even find a girl to bring home.*

GET OUT

Rhett stared at the computer screen with a satisfied grin. He was proud of what he'd accomplished with the story. Before starting the next chapter, though, he wanted to get more work done on the house. It needed his TLC. He went out to the Jeep to get the sander, oblivious as to why he hadn't already brought it in, and he began working on the living room floor. He worked for several hours, buffing the floor until it was perfectly smooth. Then he started to paint on the varnish. He didn't notice how late in the afternoon it was until his stomach growled. He stopped for a late lunch and then went right back to staining.

He got the entire room finished by 8:00 and decided to get more writing done. He didn't feel tired at all, and he wanted to take advantage of his energy boost. He skipped his medication, so he could work well into the night on his book. He figured Dave would be pleased to see how much he'd accomplished with the story. At least, he'd better be.

CHAPTER TWENTY-FIVE

Rhett wrote a long chapter on Detective Rodney Small's investigation into the murders. It was 10:30 already, but he still didn't feel tired. He felt restless. The varnish was dry enough to walk across the floor, so he went into the kitchen with industrial-strength epoxy adhesive and a box of tiles. He popped open a beer, moved the dining set into the living room, and began laying the new floor. Normally, a tiling job for a kitchen that size would take at least eight hours, but he worked faster than ever before. He was able to lay it within five. He stepped back and admired his work after setting up large box fans to dry the caulk. The room looked larger with the new floor, and it put off a happy vibe. Rhett looked at his watch. It was 4:10 a.m., and he should've gone to bed hours ago. He still didn't feel tired enough to sleep, though, so he tip-toed across the freshly laid tiles and started a pot of coffee. He opened the refrigerator to get the bread and make some toast. When he saw the leftover lasagna, he smiled to himself. The truth was, he was glad the swing broke and made her cut herself on her glass. The bitch had insulted his house.

Rhett took his coffee and toast to his desk and edited the recent chapter of *The Edge of Reason*. Then he considered the possibilities for the next part. "What trouble can Jack get into now?" he whispered to himself. He stepped inside his character's mind. What would really get him off? Something different. Something to throw the cops off—arson would do the trick.

GET
OUT

Jack went to a rowdy biker bar on the opposite end of town. He knew he wouldn't blend in, and that was exactly what he wanted. He was looking for a fight. He wanted someone to start something that only he would finish. The bikers would have no idea what hit them. It would be a test of Jack's newfound strength. He must've been putting off a vibe, though, because much to his disappointment, no one fucked with him. It didn't matter—it didn't change his plans.

Jack finished his whiskey and ordered another. He wanted to be in the perfect mood when his plans were carried out. He fully intended to enjoy the party.

Bikers were mulling around the bar, but no one paid attention to him. No one cared that he was invading their turf, and it pissed him off. They should care, and he'd soon make sure they did. He finished off a third drink and knew that it was time. Patrons were starting to leave, and that would ruin his fun. He paid his tab in cash and filed out the door behind a biker couple. They were having trouble keeping their hands off each other, so they still didn't pay him any mind.

Jack calmly walked to the Town Car and retrieved a full gas can. He then walked the perimeter of the bar, ducking into the shadows when customers were around, and doused the outside thoroughly with the fuel. He splashed both exits and all the windows too. With a smirk, he walked back to the front of the establishment and threw a lit match toward the door. He admired the flames as they licked their way around the building, exuding raw power. He quickly stepped back to avoid injury as the building went up like a tinderbox. Screams permeated the air, and he heard the bikers and staff pounding the floor to reach the exits. Then there were more screams when they discovered every exit was ablaze. A couple of the bikers took their chances against the flames, though, and ran outside. Jack watched while human comets streaked from the inferno. They dropped and rolled, as they were no doubt taught in school, but it didn't do them any good. They were burned to a crisp when their bodies and cries were finally extinguished. Charred skeletons stared at him with gaping mouths and hollowed eyes.

He heard sirens in the distance, so he jumped into the car and took off for his new home. He sang along with the radio during the drive back. "Don't Fear the Reaper" was playing on his favorite station, and he belted it out.

GET
OUT

Rhett smiled at his creation. He had been afraid to switch genres, but now he was glad that he did. He may have just found his calling. He climbed out of his desk chair to stretch his legs and get another cup of coffee, which he drank on the back porch. The woods were unusually quiet, but instead of being creepy, he found it quite peaceful. The sun would be up soon, and he could fix the front porch swing and clean up the blood and glass. *That bitch got what she deserved.*

He decided to take a quick shower. He could smell her on his clothes and skin from when she had brushed against him to kiss his cheek. He didn't want to smell her.

Ghostly whispers were telling him to *kill* her.

CHAPTER TWENTY-SIX

Rhett looked up at the bleak sky when he heard a clash of thunder. He was fixing the chain on the swing when the first raindrops fell. There was a steady breeze with the storm, so he received another refreshing shower as the rain blew into his face. He reattached the swing and climbed down his ladder. Now it was time to clean up the blood and glass. He knelt and swept the glass up with a handheld brush and dustpan. Then he poured bleach over the bloodstain and began to scrub with a coarse brush. It was easier to clean up than he'd anticipated. He took the cleaning tools inside and fetched a mop bucket full of clean water for rinsing the area. He watched as the pink rivulets ran over the side of the porch. The bleach had lightened the wood some, but it was okay since he was going to paint the flooring anyway. He'd bought red paint for both decks.

He patted the railing and said, "Soon. I'm going to paint you soon." He felt the wood warm beneath his hand. The house was telling him it was grateful.

He looked up at his bedroom window and saw a quick movement again. It didn't startle him this time, though. Somehow, he'd expected it. He gave the railing one more pat and went inside. He went straight to the kitchen to check on the caulk. It was perfectly dry, so he turned the loud fans off. He turned to look into the living room and considered applying the second coat of stain. Then, after that dried, he would apply a lacquer.

He pushed the dining table and chairs back into the kitchen and moved the living room furniture out of the way. He wished he'd waited to buy his furniture until after the floors were done, but c'est la vie. He turned on the radio, cranked it up, and got to work on the exposed flooring. When he was finished, he set the fans back out to help it dry and then sat down at his computer to work more on the book. Soon, he'd have to work on the upstairs area. He wanted to lay tile in the bathroom and paint the three rooms. He noticed the clock on his monitor, which read 3:55 p.m. He still didn't feel the least bit tired.

He looked at the screen with a smile. It was time for Jack's next exciting adventure.

GET
OUT

Jack made it home from the biker bar, feeling proud of himself, and as he pulled into the driveway, a woman caught his eye. He parked the car inside the garage, closed the door, and approached the young blonde woman, who appeared to be in her twenties. She was walking a skittish poodle, and it was after midnight—pumpkin time.

"Kind of late to be walking a dog, don't ya think?" he asked while he made his approach.

The woman immediately tensed up and looked around, but no one else was outside. They had the sense to be in bed. "Um, well, she's my sister's dog and needed to go out."

Jack casually rubbed his jawline, smelling the gasoline on his hand. "Humph. If it's your sister's dog, why isn't she doing the walking?"

Again, the woman looked around for cars, people, or any sign of life. She shifted her weight from one leg to the other and popped the knuckles on her free hand. "She's a sound sleeper, and I'm not." He could hear the tremors in her voice, and it stoked his ego.

Jack wanted to role-play with the young chippie. He drawled, "Well, this is a pretty safe neighborhood, but still, a young lady like yourself shouldn't be out here alone at night. Maybe I should walk with you just make sure you stay safe."

She laughed nervously and waved him off as he drew closer. "Oh, it's okay. I think she's done, so we're going home anyway." She tugged on the leash, but the dog didn't budge. It just stood there shivering.

He pretended to look sad. "Oh, but it's a nice night out for this time of year, so how about a walk anyway? You can tell me about yourself."

She bit her lip nervously. "Um, It's too cold, and I need to get to bed. I'm going back home tomorrow, and it's a long drive."

"Oh, so you don't live around here?" he feigned interest. He couldn't give a rat's ass where she was from. There was no way she was getting back there. "You haven't even told me your name yet."

"Yes, I'm just visiting my family. I'm on vacation, and my name is Bridget."

"It's my pleasure to meet you, Bridget. You chose an odd time of year to go on vacation."

She continued to scan the area for her escape plan. "Well, I have another one planned for summer."

Jack watched her nervously tug on her hair as she ever so slightly stepped farther away from him. The woman was foolish to think she could escape.

He wagged a finger at her. "Didn't your folks ever tell you not to talk to strangers?" he taunted.

"Yes, they did, so like I said, I should get going," she stated. Her body was quivering just as much as her voice, and he doubted the cold air had much to do with it. She spun on her heel and yanked hard on the leash to get the dog moving.

"Not much of a guard dog is it?" he asked in a lower, menacing voice this time. It made her pick up the pace, but then she froze when she heard the hammer click on his gun. A wicked grumble erupted from his chest as he mocked her. "You can't outrun a bullet, baby girl." He could tell she was thinking about it, though. "Turn around and come back. I just want to talk."

"No!" she screamed, dropped the leash, and bolted. The dog did, too, but in a different direction.

What she didn't know was that Jack was a fast runner too. With long strides, he easily caught up to her and grabbed her by the hair. He yanked hard, causing her to fall backward. He caught her with his hand over her mouth to stifle her screams while the gun pressed into her back.

"Now, let's take that walk," he growled through gritted teeth. She was feisty, though, and kept wriggling to get away. If he hadn't planned on staying in the house for a couple of days, he might have let her. *Nah. I want to have some fun.*

She kept struggling and stomped on his foot as hard as she could, almost causing him to lose his grip. *Fuck this!* He shoved her to the ground and shot her point-blank. Then, before the shot could bring anyone outside to investigate, he dragged her into the house and to the basement. She was still breathing so he finished her off with a plastic bag over her head.

Knowing his skin cells might be on her, he poured a bottle of bleach over her entire body. Then he tucked her under the laundry with the elderly couple.

"Play nice," he cooed.

CHAPTER TWENTY-SEVEN

Rhett continued to smile as he went back over the chapter. It was fun to use Bridget as the next victim in the story, and it was more fun to imagine the look on her face when she read it.

"That'll teach her to not trash talk my house," he said aloud.

Feeling restless, he decided to do some more work on the house. He felt an urgent need to use his hands. Electric energy was coursing through them, demanding action. The living room floor was dry, so he moved the furniture again and completed the other areas. Then he went upstairs to rip up the bathroom floor and lay the new tile.

By the time he finished tiling the floor, it was 4:00 in the afternoon. He couldn't believe how much he'd gotten done that day. He was working in hyper-speed, and he should've felt exhausted, but he felt great. He took a break to eat supper. He cooked a bland TV dinner and sat down to watch something on Netflix. He flipped through the choices and settled on *Criminal Minds*. Maybe an episode would inspire him for the next chapter of his book. He was engrossed in the episode when his phone rang. It was Dave.

"Hi, Dave," he answered.

"Hello, Rhett. I've been trying to get in touch with you all day, but I keep getting a message that your cell phone isn't in service. I was beginning to worry that you changed your phone number to avoid me," he said with a nervous chuckle.

"Hmm, that's odd. Anyway, you've got me now, so what's up?"

"I wanted to tell you that I've gone over what you sent to me, and it sounds good. However, you've got Jack running all over the place doing various criminal acts. Don't you think it'd be better if he stuck with one M.O.?"

Rhett felt himself grow hot with anger. He never had been good at receiving constructive criticism. "Variety is the spice of life, Dave, and I think my readers will expect it from this character. He's a wildcard, you know, and he wants to keep the cops on their toes too."

"Well, I suppose so. Just don't go too far off script, eh?"

Rhett sighed. "I'll consider reigning him in, but he has a mind of his own," he said with a lighthearted chuckle.

"Hmm, well, my advice is to stay away from too much variation," Dave told him sternly.

"Fine, Dave. Whatever you want. Now, I need to go because I have more work on the house to do, and then I want to write more so my editor will stop bitching at me." He smiled to himself as he pictured the look on Dave's face.

"Bye, Rhett," he replied in somewhat of a huff.

Rhett set his phone back down and pushed play on the episode he had been watching. A couple of minutes into it, though, his phone rang again. He growled to himself and put the show back on pause. He thought it was probably Dave with more comments, but it was an unknown number this time.

"Hello?" he answered, hoping it wasn't a telemarketer.

"Hi, Rhett. This is Bridget. I hope you don't mind me calling, but you were upset when I left yesterday, so I just wanted to check to see if you're okay."

Rhett smiled. *Speak of the devil.* "Hi. I'm doing just fine; you shouldn't have worried."

She sounded skeptical when she responded, "Oh, okay. Well, that's good." In a happier tone, she added, "I finished *Wolfsbane* last night. It was awesome, and I posted my five-star review online."

"Great. I'm glad you enjoyed it, and thanks for the review. Hey, I'm kind of in the middle of something, so I need to go."

He could hear her disappointment when she told him, "Oh, all right. I'll get out of your hair then."

"Bye," he said and quickly hung up before she could try to extend the conversation.

He turned off his laptop and went back upstairs to do more repair work. He examined the floor in the small bedroom. It was in good enough shape that he would only need to reapply lacquer. Then he looked at his bedroom floor and decided the same thing, which was good because his bedroom furniture would be too heavy and bulky to move by himself. He was just going to work around it.

He went downstairs to get the lacquer and a soda, and he noticed an open window in the living room. He couldn't remember opening it, however. He stepped near it and felt the cooling rain breeze blowing in. It was a humid day, so the breeze was refreshing. He decided to open all the windows, including the upstairs windows too, and that's when he noticed a handprint in the dust on his bedroom windowsill. He pressed a finger inside the print and found it to be cold to the touch. With a shrug, he opened the window and then applied the lacquer to both rooms and the hallway. It was 8:00 when he finished up, and he was finally feeling fatigued. He didn't feel anxious, though, so he skipped his medicine for the second time. He quickly showered and then went downstairs to sleep on the couch. The fumes from the lacquer were too strong to sleep peacefully in his bedroom.

He started to dream not long after drifting off, and he dreamed that he was Jack. He dreamed about the chapters he wrote and felt what Jack must've felt when he had killed. Strangely, he liked it. He thrived on the raw supremacy he felt as he took   lives   into   his   hands.

CHAPTER TWENTY-EIGHT

Rhett woke up around 6:00 and felt fully refreshed. It was nice to not have nightmares for a change. As disturbing as his dreams were, they still weren't bad dreams. They'd made him feel powerful, and they gave him ideas for his next chapter.

He felt a chill in the air and realized he'd left the windows open. The morning breeze was much cooler today because of the storm. He went through the house and closed all but one in the living room. Then he decided to do something he never did—he decided to go for a walk. He wanted to check out the neighborhood for the first time. He dressed in jeans, a T-shirt, and tennis shoes and headed down the street.

Maple Drive was the next street over, and it was lit up with red and blue lights. Four police cars were sitting outside of a red brick house, and residents were gawking from their lawns. He approached a young woman holding her infant.

He nodded in the direction of the spectacle and asked, "What's going on over there?"

The brunette eyed him cautiously, and he noticed when she took a step to the side. "Do you live around here? I don't recognize you."

Rhett was about to tell her where he lived, but instead, he replied, "Yeah. I just moved in on Oak Drive." He'd noticed the street above Maple the other day while on his way home from the hardware store. It boasted multiple homes for sale, so his claim was believable.

"Oh, well, welcome to the neighborhood. Unfortunately, this isn't much of a welcome, and it reflects poorly on our town, which is normally safe. There was a murder there last night, though. Beth's sister came for a visit, and she was found shot in the front yard this morning."

Rhett blanched at the news. "That's terrible. Do they have any suspects?" Before she could reply, he heard barking. A poodle was running around the front yard of the house.

"No. Beth thinks she must've walked the dog sometime late last night, and that's probably when it happened. She found her body this morning when the dog was barking to be let inside."

"How awful," Rhett mumbled as a strong sense of déjà vu overcame him. Without another word to the woman, he walked away while clenching and unclenching his fists.

He rounded the corner onto Oak Drive and headed straight. He didn't know where he was going or how far he'd go, but he needed to clear his head. The murder sounded like what he'd written yesterday. *But how can that be?* He wasn't one to believe in coincidences, but he couldn't ignore this. It was the second time something he'd written came true. *Or is it the third?* He didn't even know for sure. When he reached the opposite end of Oak Drive, he turned around and headed for home. He was remembering something else—the fire. He recalled with a grimace the details he'd read in the library's newspaper archives. He also recalled that he'd intended to leave the house. When he stepped onto Jones Drive, a powerful sense of dread filled his heart. He'd already put so much work into the house, that it made him sad to think of leaving it. However, he didn't have much of a choice. It didn't belong to him. It belonged to *them*.

CHAPTER TWENTY-NINE

After stepping inside, Rhett headed for the stairs, so he could pack his belongings up. He went to the small bedroom to get the empty moving boxes he'd neatly stacked inside the closet. He was reaching for a couple when he became lightheaded. He looked around the small room as a strange sensation overcame his body. He felt heavy, stuck, and like he was having an out-of-body experience. He stared at the walls to steady himself because he was afraid he'd topple over if he didn't. The room felt different. It felt *sad*. He could feel the house's desperate need not to be rejected by him.

He dropped the boxes and slowly walked to the corner of the room as if a large magnet was pulling him that way. He picked up the can of paint that was placed on the floor next to a tray, roller, and brush. He shook the can to make sure the blue paint was thoroughly mixed before going downstairs to fetch his ladder. When he returned, he poured some paint into the tray and dipped the roller. Carefully, he applied smooth, gentle strokes to the north wall. After covering a small area, he stepped back to admire his work and the color. His brows knitted as he stared at the wall. The paint didn't look blue at all—it looked green. It looked like the pale shade of green it had originally been. He stepped forward and applied a second coat to the same area. When he crossed the room to take another look, it was still light green. It was fresh, clean paint, but it was an undeniable pale green shade. He told himself it must be the lighting in the room and finished the painting. Blue or green, it looked better.

When he finished the bedroom, he stopped to have some lunch. He fixed a peanut butter sandwich and plopped down in front of his laptop. He opened his email and saw that he had a message from Bridget. She must've gotten his email address off his fan page because he'd not given it to her. Basically, it reiterated her phone call saying she was concerned about his well-being. She casually mentioned that she was coming back to Bondville for her cousin's wedding in two weeks and offered to stop by. She dangled a carrot—she said that they could discuss his second book, which she'd already purchased and wanted autographed.

"Humph, I don't think so, babe," he said to himself. However, after looking around the room at how nicely his efforts were paying off, he changed his mind. He typed out a short reply to her, saying that she was invited to come by during her visit.

After sorting through the remaining messages, he found a local news website and looked up the weather forecast. It was supposed to rain the next day, too, and then it was supposed to be sunny for the rest of the week. Good. He wanted to start on the back porch soon. He noticed the local headlines and the featured article on the Maple Drive murder from that morning. He read the story with interest and noticed the similarities to what he'd written yesterday.

"I'm going to have to charge the killer with copyright infringement," he mused. He took the last bite of his sandwich and set the plate off to the side so he could type. He opened his book and picked up where he'd left off.

GET
OUT

Detective Rodney Small paced his tiny office. Any minute now, the captain would rain hell's fire down on him because there was yet another killer at large. This killer, though, was an arsonist. The firebug had burned down a small but crowded biker bar, killing seventeen people.

There was also a missing person's report on his desk. Bridget Winchester, 22, was visiting her sister when she disappeared during the night. She'd apparently taken the dog out because the poodle was found outside in the morning, but there was no sign of Bridget.

A neighbor told Bridget's sister that she'd heard the dog barking around 1:30 that morning and had just assumed the poodle had gotten loose. Rodney knew of the neighborhood, which was in a nice part of town. The medium annual income for the area was $75,000. It was somewhere he'd never be able to live.

Without witnesses or a body, he couldn't tie it to the killer he was tracking, and the arson didn't seem to be related either. However, if it was, what was the motive for the fire? So far, he only had a hunch that the robberies and murders were by the same perp. He didn't have any evidence or signature to go on, though. Maybe he just wanted to believe that it was one guy so it would all be over once the guy was caught. Of course, without the homicide rate in Norfolk, he would be out of a job. It was a double-edged sword.

He went through all the case files and typed his notes into a spreadsheet so he could compare the cases yet again. There was now one incidence of arson and missing persons on top of the multiple robberies and murders. With the bar burned to the ground and no survivors, there was no way to know if a robbery had occurred there too. Also, regarding the missing woman, he doubted she would've had cash or valuables on her while walking the dog, so it was unlikely that robbery was the motive. It may turn out to be a case of sexual assault. He grunted and slammed his fist on his metal desk. He was getting nowhere.

Edna, one of the clerks, was walking by and heard his distress. "Are you okay?" she asked, popping her head inside his doorway.

"No, I'm certainly not," he grumbled without looking up. Before she could walk off, though, he said, "Hey, you're good with puzzles, and I need fresh eyes. Come here if you've got a minute."

Edna blushed and smiled. She was clearly flattered that he wanted her help. "Sure, I have time." She stepped inside the office and set her stack of folders down on the chair closest to the door. Then she leaned over his desk to see his monitor better. "Whatcha got?"

He gestured to an empty chair behind him. "Have a seat. This could take a while." She scooted the chair closer, and he pointed to the folders spread out on his desk. "You've heard about the string of robberies and murders, right?"

"Of course," she affirmed while scanning the files. "The city is quickly going to hell in a handbasket."

Rodney couldn't hide his smirk at her colorful expression. "That's one way of putting it. Anyway, I can't pin it to just one guy. There's nothing to go on. We don't have video footage, prints, DNA, or anything to tie it to someone. He, or *they*, are being too careful." He rubbed his hand over his forehead as he felt a tension headache coming on full force. He got three aspirin out of his desk drawer and swallowed them with nasty police station coffee.

She kept thumbing through his pages of notes, trying to make sense of his chicken scratch. "Hmm, well, I doubt several people are responsible because criminals, as a whole, aren't that smart. They are going to make mistakes." She glanced up at the spreadsheet and read it over too. "On the other hand, I don't see a connection either. Has anyone increased their spending habits in the area? I mean, has Joe Blow, who's never had a dime to his name, suddenly buying a new car or diamonds or something? Have you checked outside the city limits to see if robberies are increasing in other areas too? I doubt the same guy would stick to one place for long, especially now that he has dough to spend."

Rodney nodded. "We've looked for use of the stolen credit cards, but nothing has turned up there. Cash is too hard to track. I have looked at nearby counties, and the crime rates have barely fluctuated. Nothing stood out in similarity."

She scratched her arm while staring at the files again. Her face scrunched while she tried to think of something that would be useful. "I could look into recent real estate transactions to see if anything jumps out at me, such as a large cash deposit on a house or someone moving from the ghetto to the upper-east side."

"Would you? That would be great." He beamed at her, feeling a spark of hope for the first time. Anything would be helpful at this point.

"Sure. I'll get right on it, and I'll keep thinking too." She tapped her finger on her head. "It's not just a hat rack."

Rodney chuckled as she left the room. He'd always liked her and thought she was pleasant, but if she could help him crack this case, he'd have to send her a dozen red roses or something similar to show his appreciation.

He focused back on the files and his spreadsheet. "Jesus, I need a miracle to stop this maniac," he prayed.

CHAPTER THIRTY

After he sent off the chapters to Dave, Rhett felt the urge to continue painting. He grabbed the can of yellow paint, the cleaned tray, roller, and brush and headed to the bathroom. He began painting the dingy white walls a sunny yellow. He was thirsty after he finished the first small area, so he went downstairs to grab a soda. When he got back to the bathroom, he almost dropped the beverage. The wall he'd just painted yellow was white. He flicked the lights on and off several times, somehow thinking things would change, but he was still staring at a white wall. He sat on the counter and sighed.

"All right, have it your way," he groaned aloud, accepting the fact that his house knew what it wanted, and he probably couldn't fight it. He finished painting the room, and it turned out nice. It was white, but it was nice.

Tomorrow, he would need to take the sander back to the hardware store, so he looked around to make sure that he didn't need it any longer. It appeared he didn't, so he loaded it into the Jeep and locked it up. When he got back inside, he sat down on the couch with a pen and paper in hand. Sometimes, he liked to write old-school. He ended up just doodling while watching more *Criminal Minds,* though. He drew the house with its upgrades, and then he drew the landscape. When he was finished, he admired his artwork. It wasn't too bad, but he hadn't realized he was drawing tombstones in the backyard near the woods. He looked out the window and saw the setting sun in the distance. He had just enough light. . .

Rhett walked around the backyard by the edge of the woods. At first, he didn't see anything, but then he almost tripped over something. He looked down and gasped. There they were—four tombstones that he'd never noticed before. Granite headstones marked the final resting place for Rob, Diane, Patrick, and Sarah Jones. He backed away from the burial plots and turned to face the house.

"Did you do this?" he heard himself ask with trembling in his voice. "Did you kill them?" Somewhere, he heard a child's laughter.

Rhett rushed inside, turned off his laptop, then grabbed his wallet, phone, and keys, and he headed for an Inn he'd seen in town without looking   back.

CHAPTER THIRTY-ONE

Rhett flew down Route 30 on his way to the Bromley View Inn. His mind spun with images from the newspaper articles covering the fire, the feel of the locked basement door, the sounds of laughter and whispering, and finally the image of the tombstones. The skin on his arms prickled, and his eyes blurred with tears as he sped up even more. He was running, he knew, and he couldn't run fast enough. Then there were the murders in the area that matched his storyline to think about. That brought on a fierce pounding in his head and a squeezing sensation to his heart and lungs. He felt choked.

Rhett gripped his throat and yanked at the crew-neck collar on his T-shirt, gasping for air. Suddenly, he saw something out of the corner of his right eye. He slammed on the brakes as he realized it was a deer running across the highway. The loud screech of his tires and the burning smell of rubber pierced his ears and nostrils as he tried to maintain control of the Jeep. He struck the animal, and the impact made the Jeep weave sharply to the left as the front end crumpled. Rhett's immediate reaction was to jerk the steering wheel to the right, but that made matters worse, and the Jeep started to roll down the embankment. The last thing he heard was the loud pop of the airbags deploying. The last thing he felt was something striking his head while the airbag crushed his face.

GET
OUT

Rhett's eyes slowly fluttered open. He was afraid to open them too quickly because of the God-awful throbbing in his head and face. Bright overhead lights burned his pupils as he blinked rapidly to adjust. His hands flew to his face to cover them, but they were restrained by tubing, so he had to yank hard, causing a burning pain to shoot up through his arm to his shoulder. He could hear different beeping sounds and then the sound of suction as something began to squeeze his left arm.

I'm in a hospital, but why?

Rhett tried to think of the last thing he could remember, but he drew a blank. Then he heard a door open. He tried to focus his eyes on who was walking his way, but his vision was blurred.

"I'm so glad to see you're awake," a woman exclaimed with a drawl. "Let me notify the doctor, and I'll be right back to check your vitals, sweetie."

Rhett heard the door close. He looked around the room, trying to move his head, but something was holding it firmly in place. He reached with his most mobile hand and felt a cervical collar. The door opened again, and he heard hurried footsteps.

"Well, I'm glad to see you're awake, Mr. Shaw," a man said. "I'm Dr. Parks, and I've been looking after your care here."

The same nurse from before leaned over him, her frizzy black hair tumbling over her shoulders.

Rhett struggled to speak, but his throat was dry, so his words came out raspy. "Where am I?"

The doctor was the one who responded. "You are at St. Mary's Hospital. You were brought in after a car accident five days ago."

"I-I-I don't remember. What wreck?"

The nurse replied this time while checking his vitals. "The police said you hit a deer, and your vehicle rolled. You received a nasty bump to the head and face, but I'll let the doctor tell you about that."

Rhett strained to see the doctor, but his eyes were still out of focus. "My eyes are blurry," he moaned, "and my head is pounding."

The doctor cleared his throat. "Well, I imagine it would hurt after the concussion you received. The airbag almost broke your nose too. You're lucky to be alive, Mr. Shaw. It's a good thing you were wearing your safety belt." He addressed the nurse, "Carol, get him his next dose of morphine. It's been long enough since the last."

"Right away, doctor," she said, and Rhett heard her walk out the door.

"You're going to need a few days to heal here yet, and I want to order some follow-up tests before I let you go home," Dr. Parks informed him.

"Home," Rhett repeated to himself.

"I want to check your memory. Can you tell me your full name?" the doctor inquired.

Several other questions followed that one to make sure Rhett didn't suffer from amnesia. He appeared okay, but something nagged at him.

Where was I driving to? He couldn't remember what he had been doing before the accident.

CHAPTER THIRTY-TWO

Rhett spent a total of eight days in the hospital before Dr. Parks released him. He had an MRI to make sure the concussion was healing well, and he was advised to refrain from anything that would cause exertion for at least another week. The doctor gave him Vicodin to take at home for his pain.

His Jeep was totaled, but his car insurance provided an allowance for a rental. He drove home in the small Toyota Camry with a deep frown. He never liked compact cars. Laura had driven a Ford Escort, and when they went anywhere together, they had to take the Jeep. Hating the feel of the rental car, he made plans to search for dealerships in the Bondville area as soon as he got home. He'd probably buy a truck this time. It'd been Laura's idea to get the Jeep because she wanted to be ready for when they had a baby. *That dream is over.*

Rhett pulled into his driveway and stared up at the house. Eight days had been wasted, and the doctor didn't want him doing anything strenuous. He could just spend a few days writing, but the house was putting off vibes. It was begging him to get to work. He felt the energy even before he stepped inside.

He looked around the foyer and living room. The floors looked good, and everything was as he'd left it—at least as far as he could remember. He went upstairs and looked around. He'd forgotten about painting the bathroom and small bedroom. The rooms needed the trim painted white yet to go with the yellow and blue walls, respectively. He was about to leave the spare bedroom and check his when something made the hairs on his neck stand up. He looked back into the room, and a cold clamminess settled over him. There was something about the paint that he felt he should remember. He touched his fingertips to his aching head yet. They gave him a dose of Morphine at the hospital four hours ago, so he felt enough time had passed. He went downstairs and took one Vicodin. He'd never taken the drug before, and he'd been warned of the drowsiness it would cause, so he decided to hold off on repairs until he could gauge his reaction to the medicine.

He sat at his laptop and scanned through the fifty email messages he had waiting. He'd already called Dave from the hospital, but he still had messages from before their conversation to weed through. He would need to go to the Post Office tomorrow to check his P.O. Box. It was probably overflowing with mail by now. He had a message from Bridget too. She mentioned that she'd be there in a week for her cousin's wedding and was looking forward to seeing him. He wasn't in the mood to respond, so he left the message in his inbox to deal with later. He had a message from the hardware store, which he assumed was just an advertisement. However, it was a reminder that he'd not returned the floor sander. Rhett scratched his head where it was hurting as he tried to remember. *Is that where I was going? Was I on my way to return it?*

He shook his head and instantly regretted it when the throbbing intensified. The Vicodin hadn't eased the pain yet, but he was starting to feel woozy. He responded to the email, telling them about the car accident, and he instructed them to bill his credit card for the cost of the sander. He deleted most of the other messages, which were spam, and conducted his search for dealerships. He found a couple in the area to check out, so he printed off the addresses and directions. By then, his eyes were fluttering, so he shut the computer down. He wobbled when he stood up, so he turned in for the night on the couch. As he drifted off, he thought he could hear whispering upstairs.

CHAPTER THIRTY-THREE

When Rhett woke up in the early-morning hours, his head was still pounding. He took another dose of Vicodin and tried to fall back asleep, but his effort was futile. He got off the couch, stretched, and went into the kitchen to make his coffee. He had to wash the pot out from several days ago. He hadn't done the dishes before leaving the house on the day of his accident. He had only a few other items to wash, so while the coffee brewed, he tackled the chore.

He filled his largest mug to the rim and sat down at his desk. After his laptop warmed up, he checked the weather report and then the local news for the past week. He found the article on his accident. The police reported that the Jeep struck a deer on Route 30 and overturned several times. It mentioned Rhett's injuries, claiming he was seemingly struck in the head by the floor sander, which was in the passenger seat.

The Vicodin was kicking in faster this time, and his eyes became droopy as he read. He turned on *CSI Miami* and plopped back down on the couch. He noticed his notepad in front of him on the coffee table and picked it up to look at his drawing. A scowl deepened the lines in his forehead as he studied the tombstones he'd sketched. He couldn't recall why he'd put them in as part of the landscape. He usually wasn't that morbid, but then again, he was killing off people in his latest book, so maybe he had a dark side after all. He dropped the notepad to the floor as sleep overpowered him.

He dreamed that he was walking through the house, admiring his renovations, when there was a knock on the front door. He looked out the cut-out window and saw Bridget standing on the porch. He let her inside with a mumbled greeting, and she immediately scanned the living room area.

"You're doing a pretty good job with the repairs. It doesn't look like a dump anymore."

Rhett clenched his hands into tight fists as he tried hard to control his temper. It was beyond rude to invite herself into his house and then insult it. Yes, it had been in poor shape when he moved in, but still, her attitude was rather off-putting.

"Can I see the upstairs? I've never been up there."

Humph. So you can trash it too? Instead of saying what he was thinking, he just nodded. He followed her up the stairs while his eyes burned a hole into her back. She'd probably find something up there to bitch about too. She went into the small bedroom first.

"That's a pretty color you chose for the walls. What color was it in here?" she acted truly interested.

"Pale green," he mumbled.

"I like the blue better," she replied as if she thought he actually cared what she preferred. She went into the bathroom next. "Yellow? It surprises me that a single man would choose such a bright color."

Rhett ran a hand over his jaw, which was clenching so tightly it made his teeth hurt. "I've not started on the rest of the upstairs, so why don't we go back down to the living room?" he seethed.

Her eyes went wide at his tone. "Umm, okay."

He motioned to the staircase. "After you."

She stepped around him and began to descend the stairs. She lost her footing, though, and tumbled down the rest of the way, striking her head against the wall and then the floor as she crumpled into a heap at the bottom. Rhett slowly walked down the steps, wearing a menacing smile, and stood over her lifeless body. He hadn't touched her, so the police would just chalk it up as an unfortunate accident, but he knew better. He knew it was the house. It didn't like her pissy attitude toward it either.

"I know," he said in a soothing tone and patted the wall, "She was a bitch and got what she deserved."

Rhett's eyes flew open, and he sat upright so quickly, that the pounding inside his head started in again. His hands flew to his temples while he rode out the waves of torture. He wasn't psychic, and he wasn't superstitious, but the dream had been a warning. He shouldn't let her come over again. It wouldn't be safe.

CHAPTER THIRTY-FOUR

Since Rhett was awake, he decided to write more. He read back over the last chapter to reacquaint himself with the story and to put himself in the moment. He decided to continue the story with more about the detective.

GET
OUT

Rodney stopped off at MJ's Tavern after finally leaving the police station. He took the files with him, though, in case he couldn't sleep that night either. He hadn't had a decent amount of rest since the killer had first struck several days ago, and he didn't see that changing until the bastard was locked up. He knew the retired detective sitting at the bar, so he took the empty stool next to him.

"Detective Small," the man mumbled when he looked up.

"Hi, Jim. How's retirement treating you?" Rodney asked him.

The man saluted Rodney with his empty glass, swirling the ice around. "Not bad. If I said I missed the job, I'd be lying. On the other hand"—he looked down at his empty glass—"being home with the missus every day is a little trying at times. She even told me to get a girlfriend."

Rodney almost spat out his beer when he laughed. He'd never gotten married, never even came close to it, but he'd heard all the stories and all the jokes.

"You're one of the lucky ones, Small. Tell me, though, how did you manage to avoid taking the plunge for this long?"

Rodney opened his arms in a shrug. "I guess no one would have me. The dangerous job, the late hours, the stress. . . Hell, I've never even had the time to find out if there was a woman out there for me."

Jim laughed while summoning the bartender to fill him up. "Well, if you've made it this far on your own, why mess with it?"

"I don't have time to even think about that. I want to pick your brain on my current case," Rodney opened up.

"Always follow the evidence," Jim recommended and held his full glass up in a salute.

Rodney took a deep breath to calm his nerves. "That's the problem, Jim. He's not leaving any evidence. There aren't any eyewitnesses, there are no fingerprints, no DNA, no signature to follow. He's not leaving breadcrumbs anywhere."

Jim cocked his head and slanted his eyes. "Do you really believe that? Do you really believe that a psychopathic killer is so smart that he isn't going to fuck up somewhere?"

Rodney finished off his beer and slammed the bottle down on the countertop, catching the eye of the bartender. She grabbed another beer for him and slid it across the counter. He tapped the fingers of his free hand on the bar.

"I'd love to believe that all the bad guys eventually fuck up, giving us an opening to catch them, but of course I know that's not reality," Rodney's tone let on that he felt beat.

"You know, Small, I've taken up fishing lately, and some days, I catch a whole bunch, but most days I have to throw a wider net."

Rodney cocked his head at the retiree. "And what the hell are you trying to say?"

Jim frowned because Rodney hadn't understood the message. After taking a healthy swig of his drink, he replied, "What I'm saying is this. You are looking for a specific kind of perp in a specific area, whereas what you need to do is cast a wider net. For all you know, he could be the pastor's son or the quiet neighbor next door. Look at everybody as a suspect and then find the reasons why they couldn't be. Just make sure that the reasons are tangible and not based on a hunch." He paused long enough to take another drink of his Scotch. "I, of course, assume you've already dipped into NCIC to look for similar crimes. Have you considered asking the FBI for help?"

"Yes, I have, but the captain said when and if they get called in, it will be by him."

Jim downed the rest of his drink and stood up to leave. "Well, keep in mind what I told ya. Look where you've never dared to look before. It just might help. Take care." He gave Rodney two pats on the back as he walked past his stool.

"You too, Jim. You too." Rodney pushed away the rest of his beer and left as well. He wanted to go home and look through the files again. Maybe the dead had something in common. If he could find a link, he could find a path to the killer's doorstep.

GET
OUT

Rhett wanted to go back over the chapter before he sent it off to Dave. He also wanted to add some material on Jack. However, his most pressing concern was finding something to eat. He'd been on IV fluids and then hospital food, so he needed something real to eat. He walked into the kitchen and heated up some beef vegetable soup after throwing out rotten food from the refrigerator. He'd go to IGA after the dealership in the morning. He looked at the clock on the stove and saw that it was 10:30 p.m. He had no idea how long he'd napped, but he felt rested enough to write a little more before turning in for the night.

He took his soup and sat down at the laptop. Instead of opening the book, though, he went back to the two local dealership websites and looked at the trucks they had in inventory. Both sites had a test drive scheduling app, so he set up an appointment for 9:30 at the Ford dealership. If he didn't like the trucks there, he'd go to the Chevrolet dealership. He noticed a link at the bottom of the screen for RV sales, and he clicked on it. He'd never thought about owning an RV before, but now that he had the time to travel, it might be fun to just drive all over and see the country. Maybe he'd visit the places he described in his books. Of course, he'd need to finish remodeling the house first, but that should only take another week or two if he disregarded the doctor's orders and got back to work. He grabbed his notepad, turned to a clean page, and listed what he wanted to do yet. He needed to repaint the master bedroom, but there wasn't any hurry. He needed to paint the outside and refinish the back deck. He needed to replace the shingles on the roof, but that would have to wait until he was off the Vicodin. Eventually, he may want to finish the basement or at least put in a better workbench, but that could wait. He was still thinking about carpeting the stairs and putting down an area rug too.

The more he jotted down on the list, the more his heart raced. He felt the urge to get busy, so after he finished the soup, he went up to his bedroom and started painting. The walls had been a light blue shade, but the color he put on now was royal blue. It reminded him of the Caribbean waters he'd seen with Laura when they were on their honeymoon. He could never go back there without her, but he could have a piece of it here. He picked up one of the framed photographs he had of them on the beach in St. Thomas. The Caribbean Sea blended perfectly with the new walls, and he was sure that Laura was smiling down from heaven.

He looked at his alarm clock on the nightstand. It was 12:30 a.m. He still didn't feel sleepy, though, so he went back to his laptop to write more of Jack's story.

CHAPTER THIRTY-FIVE

Jack slept in late Monday morning. The king-size bed was just too comfortable to leave. When he finally forced himself to get up, he took a long hot shower. It was without a doubt the best shower he'd ever had. The water stayed hot, and no one was yelling at him to get out. There was clean water, a clean stall, and no bugs were around.

He fixed a hearty breakfast of bacon and eggs after the refreshing wash and sat down in front of the TV. He channel-surfed until he came across the local news. A hearty laugh escaped his thin lips when he saw the coverage on the fire and missing blonde. Police had no suspects in either case and were pleading for eyewitnesses to come forward.

"Bridget Thomas, it was a pleasure to meet you," he mumbled to himself and instinctively looked at the floor. It was going to be a frigid day, barely reaching 25 degrees, but he knew the bodies would start smelling up the house soon. He decided to use the old lady's laptop to search the apartment listings in the area and nearby cities. He could use a change of scenery from Norfolk. He could use new hunting grounds.

He found a listing for a new condo unit that was still filling up in Virginia Beach, which was seventeen miles away. He chuckled to himself. *I always wanted to live by the beach*. The complex was only three blocks from the Virginia Beach Boardwalk, which could be lucrative for him. It was likely to be expensive, but thanks to the elderly couple and his new career, he could afford it. He wrote down the realtor's information and noted that there was an open house today starting at 11:30. He cleaned up his dishes, dressed for the weather in one of the old man's sweaters, which fit him decently enough, and drove to the condo unit. Sea Harbor sounded like a beautiful place to live.

It was snowing during his drive to the open house, and everyone was slamming on the brakes, so he had to be extra careful. He couldn't get involved in an accident in the stolen car. That wasn't in his plans. Thanks to the GPS in the vehicle, he found the condo unit without any trouble and pulled into the parking lot. He quickly located the correct building and climbed the stairs to the second floor. He rapped lightly on the door and waited for someone to answer.

"Come on in," a portly man greeted him, and Jack immediately recognized him as the realtor. "Welcome to Sea Harbor, where every day is an escape from the mundane."

"Hello," Jack replied and scanned the open living room. *Nice digs.*

"Let's look around, shall we?" the realtor asked with a smile that Jack wanted to punch off the man's face. Morning people got on his nerves.

"Lead the way," he mumbled.

"I'm the realtor, Joe Brooks. And you are?"

Jack gave the name on a fake ID he had. "I'm Tom Wilson."

"Nice to meet you, Tom. Let me show you the master bedroom first."

Jack had never rented an apartment with two bedrooms before. He decided that he could make the smaller room a weight-lifting area. He'd need to build up his strength for his new career as a professional thief.

"So, what do you think?" Joe asked when he'd shown the entire place. "It's a nice neighborhood and close to the beach."

"Yeah, it's nice. How much is it?"

The realtor looked away first, then told him, "It's $180,000, but of course financing is available, and you'll be on the beach."

"You don't have to sell me on it. How does this work? I've only rented before," Jack explained.

The man's eyes bulged. He was probably calculating his commission for the tenth time. "Well, all right then. Let's sit down and go over the paperwork." With a bounce in his step, he led Jack to the kitchen where a small table was set up. It had numerous files stacked on it and a couple of pens. He scooted the folders over and gestured to the chair. "Have a seat."

Jack pulled out the folding chair and sat down across from Joe. The realtor pulled several pages out of the file folders and neatly stacked them.

"Here are the application forms. Let me just grab my laptop, so I'll be able to check your credit," Joe said and reached for a briefcase underneath the table. He pulled out a small laptop and turned it on.

Jack felt overwhelmed as he looked over the paperwork. He'd never filled out anything more complicated than a job application before. He started with the first page because it was the easiest. He filled out his contact information using the fake name, social security number, and address.

"This is a lot of paperwork, and I don't think I'll need to fill all of it out. I won't need the financing. I can pay with a cashier's check," Jack told the realtor.

The man blanched, and he dropped his pen. He grunted when he bent over to pick it up from the floor, and Jack saw beads of perspiration on the man's forehead. "You want to pay for it all in one lump sum? Is that correct?"

Jack smiled as politely as he could. "Yeah. I hate to pay interest when I don't need to. My folks just passed away, God rest their souls, and they left me enough money to buy a place outright. I just don't want a house to keep up with because I like to travel," he lied with as much sincerity as he could muster.

"It's nice to not have to mow the grass or shovel snow too," Joe replied with a grin. "I'll tell you what, I can probably get $5,000 taken off the asking price if you pay in full. I'm sure the contractor will agree. Let me give him a quick call while you fill out the other papers." He pulled his cell phone out of his suit pocket before Jack could object, and he walked away from the table to make the call in private.

Jack worked on filling out the papers he comprehended, setting the others off to the side. Soon, Joe returned with another big smile.

"Done. The contractor agreed to knock $5,000 off the price. Are you done with the paperwork?"

"No," Jack admitted, "I'm not sure about these papers here." He pushed the stack toward the realtor, who then went over each one with an explanation and got Jack to sign.

"You mentioned a cashier's check earlier. Is that something you can do today?" Joe asked with hope filling his voice.

Jack nodded. "I saw a bank down the street, so I can go get it right now"—he rose from the chair—"I'll be right back. Now, who do I make it out to?"

Joe cleared his throat and rose to open the door for Jack. "Umm, you'll make it out to Colter Construction. That's C-o-l-t-e-r."

Jack nodded again and left the condo. He then drove up the street to the US Bank branch and took in the checkbook belonging to the elderly couple. Without question, the teller-in-training sold him the cashier's check for a $5 fee. In truth, Jack had enough cash to pay for the cashier's check after emptying the couple's fat bank account, but he needed that money for other expenses. This way, too, he got to screw US Bank, which had denied him for a personal loan before.

After he left the bank, he threw the rest of the checkbook away into the nearest trash bin. He'd worn his winter gloves and left no prints.

He drove back to his new home and found Joe turning away a middle-aged couple who'd come to check out the open house.

"I'm sorry, but here's the new owner now," he said and pointed to Jack. "And of course, there are still units available in the next building. They're a little smaller but just as nice." The couple waved him off, though, and left without turning back.

Jack handed Joe the cashier's check. "Is there anything else I have to do?"

Joe handed him two keys to the unit and smiled. "No, that's it for the paperwork. Let me give you a couple of business cards for moving companies though." He dug into his breast pocket and pulled out three cards. "I've talked to satisfied customers of all three of these services."

Jack took the cards and shook the realtor's meaty hand. "Thank you. I'll give them a call. I'm anxious to move in."

Joe packed up his table, chairs, and laptop and backed out into the hallway. "I'll leave you to get acquainted with your new home. Welcome to the neighborhood, Mr. Wilson. Be sure to call me if you need anything else."

Jack nodded once in the man's direction. "Will do." He shut and locked the door and then ran like a child through his new place.

He pulled the business cards out of his pants pocket and threw them in the little trash can the realtor had left in the bathroom. He only had to get his clothes from the elderly couple's house. He was going to go buy only brand-new furniture—something he'd never had before. He was also going to call his landlord and tell him to shove the roach motel and all of its contents up his fat ass.

"On second thought, I think I'll let him figure that out on his own when I don't show up with the rent in a few days," he said aloud and chuckled. It gave him a good idea, too. It was time for a new identity—he deserved a new life. He pulled out his phone to call the ex-convict who made his new living by making fake IDs and forging documents. Jack could trust him because he trusted Jack to keep his secret from the parole board.

CHAPTER THIRTY-SIX

Pleased with his chapter, Rhett sent it off to Dave and lay on the couch to rest. He wouldn't be able to sleep upstairs yet because of the paint fumes. He set his alarm for 7:30, which would give him five hours to sleep. He dreamed the same thing he'd dreamed earlier—Bridget came by and ended up dead. Then he didn't dream at all.

The alarm on his phone woke him promptly at 7:30, and he got up with a big stretch and a couple of yawns. He slowly climbed the stairs, used the bathroom, and climbed into a hot shower. His dream came back to him, and he tried to wash the memory away. He didn't care for the woman, but he didn't wish her harm either. He figured the dreams were just a result of his book and overactive imagination. That made him wonder what kind of dreams Stephen King had.

After two cups of coffee, Rhett left to go to the dealerships. He couldn't wait to get behind the wheel of something masculine. At the Ford dealership, he test drove a couple of trucks before he found and settled on a 2017 midnight blue F-150. He signed the papers and ditched his rental car.

Rhett stopped off at the grocery store and picked up some essentials before heading home. He loved the feel of the truck as it sped down the highway toward the house. He kept a watchful eye out for deer, though. *Fool me once. . .*

When he got home, he put the groceries away and then walked through the house, looking for his next project. He decided to lay the carpet on the stairs, which required another trip to the hardware store.

The parking lot was barely full when he got there. The same cashier who'd rented the sander to him was working in flooring today.

"Mr. Shaw, it's good to see you again. I heard about your car accident and was concerned. Thank you for handling the payment for the sander, though."

"Thanks. I want to look at carpet samples and area rugs today," Rhett informed the clerk.

"Sure. I can help with that. Did you get your address figured out by the way?"

Rhett looked at the young man with anger burning behind his eyes and addressed him by name when he said, "Look, Scott, I don't know what your problem is, but I know my address. I always have. I live at 100 Jones Drive. Now, can you help me, or do I need to get the manager?"

Scott's face turned red, and he stammered a quick reply. "Um...s-s-sure. I can help you. I'm sorry. Someone must've rebuilt a house on the old lot, and I just didn't know it."

Rather than argue with the kid, who was probably making minimum wage, Rhett nodded. "Yeah, I suppose so."

Scott pointed to their left. "One aisle over is our collection of area rugs. You can pick out the one you like, and then we'll match the carpeting."

Rhett pulled out his paper full of measurements and walked to the rugs. He was at the store for thirty-five minutes finding the perfect rug and carpet to compliment it. He chose deep shades of red to blend in with the paint he'd chosen for the outside trim and decks. Scott helped him load the materials into the back of the new truck.

"This is a nice truck!" he remarked. "I drive an old Chevy pick-up myself"—he looked down at his feet—"I want to apologize again about the confusion with your address. I didn't mean to upset you."

"It's okay," Rhett replied and shook the man's hand. "It was just a misunderstanding."

"I'm sure it is, and I hope we can continue being your go-to hardware store," Scott mumbled with a blush.

Rhett smiled and nodded. "I'm sure I'll be back soon for shingles. I'm going to redo the roof after I finish with painting."

"All right. We'll see you soon then," Scott said and walked off with a wave.

Rhett drove home and carefully carried the rug and carpet rolls inside. It was difficult to do by himself, though, and he got dirt on the end when he dropped the rolled-up area rug.

He cleaned the dirt off, moved his furniture out of the way, laid the rug in place, and then pushed the furniture back into place. It looked good. He could even feel the house's admiration.

He decided to lay the carpeting on the stairs next. The throbbing was gone from his head, and he wanted to take full advantage of it.

CHAPTER THIRTY-SEVEN

Rhett's knees and hands were aching when he finished laying the carpet, which gave him the perfect excuse to write. He checked his email first and responded to Bridget's last message. He told her that he'd be too busy with remodeling the house for a visit, so she shouldn't stop by. He mentioned, however, that they could maybe get together the next time she was around. Hopefully, that'd be good enough for her, and she wouldn't push.

He opened his book document, stretched out his sore fingers, and began to type.

GET
OUT

Rodney went into work an hour early and was grateful that there weren't any new homicide reports on his desk. Maybe his killer even took a day off now and then.

He laid out the files and his notes and poured over them again while sipping his coffee. He had stared at them until he fell asleep last night, but he didn't see anything new. He couldn't see any connections between the victims or areas of town that had been hit. Then there was the random fire. Except for the seventeen counts of manslaughter, there was no connection. He supposed the killer had robbed the joint and then burned it to the ground to keep the bikers from coming after him, but that was just a theory. It was a rough bar, and he didn't think the clientele would've let someone just walk out of there with their belongings even if he had a gun. Hell, they were usually packing guns themselves. *So, did he even get inside the bar, or did he just burn it down?*

"Good morning, Rodney," Edna called out while she hung her coat up on the coat rack by the entrance.

"Good morning, Edna," he replied. He heard the clickety-clack of her heels as she walked toward his office.

"Have you come up with anything on your case?" she inquired with concern.

"No, I'm falling flat on my face with this one," he grumbled.

"Well, I'm going to look into real estate purchases and upgrades like I mentioned yesterday. Hopefully, something will turn up." She pulled a pen from behind her ear and wrote something down on her palm.

Rodney was glad to have her lending enthusiasm toward solving the case. He sure as shit wasn't getting anywhere by himself. There used to be a couple of other homicide detectives in the department, but one left for new stomping grounds, while the other retired. The chief of police didn't want to spend the funding to hire new detectives for the department. He said that Rodney could recruit floater detectives if he needed to, but currently, there weren't any available. Today, he'd check to see if that had changed. Maybe someone was free to help out now. He wrote a note to himself on his blotter to speak to the captain about it. He didn't relish the idea of going back into the man's office with his hat in his hand, but what choice did he have? He'd forgotten Edna was standing in the doorway until she cleared her throat.

"Sorry, Edna. My mind was wandering off. Please do that, and let me know what you find out. Thanks by the way."

Edna's cheeks turned rosier than they already were from the cold. "You're welcome. I'm glad to have something exciting to do around here for a change." She smiled and clickety-clacked her way back to her desk.

Rodney's desk phone buzzed, making him twitch enough to spill a little of his coffee into his lap. *Of all the days to wear khaki pants.* He looked at the display and saw the captain's name. *Shit.* It was time to take his lumps. He grabbed his legal pad and pen and trudged to the office of Captain Roger Clark.

"Sit down," he was ordered as soon as he stepped inside the doorway. "What the hell is going on with the case, Small? I've got the chief of police pissing down my back over this, and I gotta tell you, I hate the smell of piss."

Rodney looked down at his lap, feeling his cheeks burn from embarrassment. "I know, sir, and I'm sorry. This killer is smart, though, and he's not leaving any clues. I was planning on asking you today if I could get another detective or two to help me with this."

"Is that right? It just so happens that I checked on that yesterday, but no one is available. All the floaters are already assisting task forces in other departments. I put the word out to send any available people this way, though, if someone's schedule opens up. In the meantime, what are you doing?"

Rodney slowly swung his head side to side while he wrung his hands in his lap. "I'm doing all that I can with this. Even Edna offered her eyes yesterday, and she's calling realtors in the area to see if anyone has purchased a house or a nicer apartment with cash."

The captain rubbed the gray stubble on his chin and leaned back in his leather chair. "Hmm...I'm not sure how I feel about a clerk helping you out, but since she's just doing research, I suppose it's okay. Good idea too. Someone suddenly flushed with cash will be no doubt spending it. Check with the drug unit to see if there have been any unusual buys on the streets. He might be frequenting dealers more often or even prostitutes too."

"I'll do that as soon as I leave your office, sir."

The captain waved a dismissive hand at him. "No time like the present. Let me know what you find out. I need to be in the loop at all times."

"Yes, sir," Rodney promised as he stood to leave. Once he stepped outside into the bullpen, he heaved a sigh of relief. It could've gone much worse.

CHAPTER THIRTY-EIGHT

After he sent the chapter to Dave, Rhett grabbed a beer and went outside to sit on the refurbished porch swing. It was below freezing, but he wore his coat and didn't mind the frigid air. He looked around the porch and out into the yard, which seemed to glow beneath the full moon. It looked like a scene he had described in his first novel. Of course, that passage had a werewolf in it, and while he was certain there weren't any werewolves running around his yard, he did feel something sinister. It seemed to be coming from the house. He looked through the window at the new lamp on his desk. Suddenly, the light went out. *Shit. That's a new lamp and a new bulb.*

With a heavy sigh, he went back inside, flipping on the overhead light as he walked through the foyer to the living room. He checked the filament in the light bulb and saw that it was already burned out.

"Now, how in the hell did that happen?"

He would need to flip the circuit breaker and then check the lamp wiring. He didn't relish the idea of going to the basement, but he stuck a slim flashlight into his pocket, unlocked the door with the skeleton key, and descended the stairs into its creepy depths.

He opened the circuit box, flipped the breaker to the living room, and went upstairs into the darkened room with the flashlight on. He made his way into the kitchen with the lamp and his toolbox in hand.

When he'd gone to trade school for carpentry, he'd picked up some electrical classes too. Hoping he remembered enough, he opened up the lamp and inspected the wires. He used his voltage tester, and everything appeared to be correct. He checked the area around where the bulb met the fixture insulation for signs of heat damage and saw slight scorch marks, so he screwed in a new bulb with a lower wattage. He plugged the lamp in and went downstairs to turn the breaker back on. Before he went up the steps, though, he heard something that made him pause—he heard scratching at the basement window.

Rhett hurried back up the steps and locked the basement door. Then he checked the front and back patio doors to make sure that they were also locked. He didn't have any bushes near the house, so he didn't know what had made the scratching noise, but he wasn't going to let whatever it was walk into his house. He told himself it was probably just a stray cat, but somehow, he knew it was something more than that. He knew it was something *sinister*. His skin prickled and the hairs on his neck stood up.

His heart was racing, so he decided to put it to good use. He started to write another tale for Jack, hoping it would take his mind off other things.

CHAPTER THIRTY-NINE

Jack met with Eric Cooper and purchased his new driver's license and Social Security card for $10,000. Damon Bradshaw was now one of his identities. He was even provided with a fake high school diploma and resume.

Eric joked, "Congratulations! You're now a high school graduate!" Of course, that didn't matter now with Jack's new career path.

"Won't Mom be proud?" he mused.

Eric put down the newspaper he was reading and said, "Whatever you're up to, I hope I don't read about it in the paper." His serious expression cracked with a big smile. "I'm just kidding. Good luck in not getting caught, man."

Jack pointed a finger at his friend. "Hey, you too. I may need your services again in the future if I suddenly need to disappear."

Eric popped his knuckles and flashed a toothy grin. "Well, now that's my specialty."

"I'll keep that in mind," Jack said and gave the man a fist bump. He let himself out of the grimy apartment and headed to the furniture store four blocks over.

He was looking around when two different members of the sales staff pounced on him with a million questions. He held up a hand to fend them both off.

"Whoa! I only need one of you to help me," he chastised them and then pointed to the woman. "You. You can help me."

"Great! Let's see what we can find for you," she exclaimed while the man scowled and stormed off, mumbling something incoherent.

Jack rubbed his hands together and took the expansive showroom in with a huge smile. This was going to be the best day of his life! He walked around with the sales lady and picked out furniture for the dining room, living room, and bedroom. He would have to go elsewhere for his weightlifting equipment, but there was no rush. Hauling corpses around was already building his strength. He arranged for immediate delivery to the new condo, even though it cost him a lot extra.

CHAPTER FORTY

Rhett stood and stretched after sending the chapter off to Dave. With a yawn, he looked at his watch and saw that it was already midnight. *Time does fly.* He grabbed his pillow and headed up the stairs to his bedroom. The new couch was comfortable, but he needed to stretch out in his bed again.

As he lay in bed, he realized it was too quiet. He didn't miss the city noise, but he was growing tired of hearing only his thoughts and the rattle of the furnace at night. Tomorrow, he'd buy ceiling fans for the bedroom and the living room. He'd also buy paint for the living room walls. Since they weren't in bad shape, his original plan was to leave them white; however, now he wanted them to blend with the furniture and carpet and give the room a more relaxing vibe. He'd go with taupe paint and add a red patterned border at the top. He thought about getting the curtains while he was out too. The paint would have to dry first, of course, but it would be one more thing to cross off his to-do list. He smiled while staring up at the ceiling as he thought about how nicely the house was coming together. Weird noises and odd happenings aside, it was finally starting to feel like home.

Rhett slept for only five hours off and on before giving up and getting out of bed. He took a shower, made his coffee, and sat on the porch swing, taking slow slips while the sun began to rise. He could already tell it was going to be a two-cup morning. He looked out at the yard and the fog swirling around it. It made him think of *Wolfsbane* again. He hadn't checked his royalty reports lately, so he added the task to his mental checklist.

He began to walk around the yard, visualizing flowerbeds and even a vegetable garden off to the side. He walked the perimeter of the house, and when he reached the back, he considered putting in a picket fence. He hadn't had a dog for several years because when Laura's Lhasa Apso passed away at the age of fifteen, she was too heartbroken to get another. That was one month before her own passing. He looked up at the sky and pictured Laura holding the dog while looking down at him. *I lost both my girls in just a month. Unfair!* Yes, a dog might be just what he needed to pull himself out of his funk.

He continued walking around the backyard, planning on the height of the fence and where to put in some shrubs and maybe another flowerbed, when he noticed something. The patch of fog had lifted enough to show him the four tombstones he'd forgotten about. But that wasn't what had made his heart stop for a beat and a cold sweat to break out. He couldn't breathe or move as he stood staring at the swirling apparition of a little girl standing over one of the tombstones.

The spirit looked up at the house, back down at the tombstone, and then at Rhett. Her expression changed completely when she stared at him. Her hollow eyes seemed to grow blacker, and she pointed an accusing finger at him. Her long, transparent hair swirled around her shoulders in perfect rhythm with the mist that was still clinging to the frosty air. The eerie scene kept Rhett frozen in place while his mind tried to process what he was seeing. He knew it wasn't from the Vicodin because the last dose he'd taken was a couple of days ago. It wasn't from a lack of sleep either, and he pinched himself to be sure he was awake now.

"I'm sorry for what happened to you, Sarah," he mumbled when he found his voice.

The phantom child jabbed her finger at him. "Leave," she said firmly but quietly.

"Sarah, I understand this was your house, and I'm sorry for what happened to you and your family, but it's my home now," he explained to the ghost at the same time he questioned his sanity.

She slowly shook her head, with her hair still swirling around her shoulders in an eerie dance, and told him loudly this time, "Leave! It doesn't want you!"

Rhett cocked his head and spoke in a soothing tone as if he were trying to calm down a living, breathing child. "Sarah, the house likes me. It likes the repairs I'm making. I can feel its joy while I—"

"No! You have to leave," she pleaded in her hushed voice again. She sounded like she was on the brink of tears.

"Why?" he asked softly.

The ghost child looked up at the house again before she answered him. "Please, you have to listen to me. You have to leave immediately," she begged in a child's tearful, whiney voice. Then she whispered, "It gets angry, and then it consumes you."

Before Rhett could even form a response, they both heard a child's laughter. It was the same laughter he'd heard at least twice already.

"I have to go," the spirit told him tenderly and stepped into the woods where she disappeared within the fog, still clinging to the trees. He heard her laughter now too.

Rhett listened until he couldn't hear the children any longer. Then he approached her tombstone, where she'd been floating, and put down some budding wildflowers he'd found nearby.

He mumbled to himself, "I'm sorry, Sarah. I'm sorry that you can't see my bond with the house"—he turned to face his home—"You just don't understand that the house is a part of me now."

CHAPTER FORTY-ONE

In a state of shock, Rhett walked with halting steps back to the house and clung to the railing as he slowly climbed the steps. Every movement was mechanical, and his breaths were shallow to the point of his chest aching. He didn't hear the laughter anymore; he just heard his heart's rapid pounding.

He'd never believed in ghosts, witches, werewolves, vampires, or anything paranormal before. Like many writers before him, he just made up such beings in the stories he spun. Laura, on the other hand, had confided in him, when he'd first started writing his book, that she'd had a visit from her dead grandmother on more than one occasion. He'd pretended to believe her, so her feelings wouldn't get hurt, but he'd laughed on the inside. He wouldn't laugh anymore. There was no denying what he'd just seen outside—he'd talked to Sarah's spirit.

He began to type furiously in the search engine. Several pages about specters soon populated the screen, and he began frantically clicking. There were multiple websites full of stories about ghostly encounters and haunted houses. Some people claimed that the ghosts were dead relatives who let them live in peace, while others claimed a grim evil was inhabiting their home and trying to force them out. Rhett paid close attention to those stories. However, he just couldn't imagine that the little girl, who was robbed of her life so early, was an evil entity. Her demands for him to leave the house had been more of a warning than a threat. She'd said the house would get angry and consume him. *But why? Why would the house turn on me when I've shown it so much love?*

He looked up the news story on the house fire again. He found a couple of mentions online, but nothing was as in-depth as the newspaper clippings he'd found in the library archives. There was a photo of the fire, though, and the flames were enveloping the house. Rhett looked up at the ceiling and all around the room. *Is that what she'd meant? Did the house get angry at her family and kill them?* But that wouldn't make sense unless the house had been possessed while they lived there. *If the Jones family isn't possessing the house now, who is?*

Rhett ran a new search. He looked up ways to find out who all of the previous homeowners were. Several articles came up explaining how to run a search on a home's history. He chose the one listed first and waited for the site to load. A nervous excitement ran through his blood and made his fingers tingle. He liked the idea of learning more about his house.

When the site finally fully loaded, he discovered that he'd have to seek the help of the county recorder to learn the house's deed history. He didn't like the idea of having to talk to someone in person, especially if he or she was also going to bring up the fire, so he found an email address to write to instead. The clerk's name was Mary Swann. He opened his email and composed his message. He wrote that he was interested in the property and wanted to know its history before he tried to purchase it. Of course, he didn't say anything about already having moved in.

He sent off the email and opened his book. The blank page was an abominable sight, though, and his mouth went dry as he tried to form words to fill it. His mind wasn't on writing. It was on haunted houses. He wasn't afraid of the house, but some of the shit that had already happened scared the hell out of him—like being locked in the basement. *Why would the house do that?*

Rhett was feeling out of sorts, so he took his Xanax for the first time in days. Maybe he should call the doctor to see if it would help protect him against ghosts. If something sinister had killed the Jones family, what would it do to him?

An idea came to him, and he began to write. He had a story about Jack's demons to tell.

CHAPTER FORTY-TWO

Jack bought groceries, consisting of quality food for a change, and headed home to meet the delivery men from the furniture store. The condo came with a stove and running refrigerator, so he bought frozen foods. The men were already there when he arrived, but he didn't care. He paid a lot of money to have his items immediately, so if they had to wait a few minutes on him, so be it. He opened the door and stepped out of the way, so they could bring in the sofa first.

One of the men told him, "You bought some really nice pieces, man. I think you'll be happy with it for a long time."

Jack couldn't help but wonder if the store paid him extra for the advertising. "Thanks," he said and stood back to admire the couch. "I think I'd rather have it along this wall over here." He nodded with his head where he wanted it to go. "Then the recliner can go over there, and the TV can go across from it."

"Sure, no problem. We'll set it up in whatever way makes you most comfortable," the other man mumbled. Then they both left the condo to get more items from the truck.

Jack sat on the new sofa and sighed while rubbing his hand over the soft, supple leather. "This is the life."

He closed his eyes to visualize how the room would look with everything set up, but then his phone rang and disturbed the image. With a grunt, he pulled it out of his pocket. It was his boss calling.

"Hello, Don," he greeted the man.

"Jack, how are you? Are you feeling well enough to get your ass back to work?" Don inquired in a grouchy tone.

Jack chuckled into the phone. "I guess I forgot to tell you I'm not coming back. I quit."

Don's anger flared, and he demanded, "What? What the hell do you mean you quit? You need to give me a two-week notice, or I'll never give you a good reference."

Jack laughed harder at the threat. "Shit, I don't give a rat's ass about a reference from you, man. Besides, I've already got a new gig." He ended the call and blocked the man's number. He didn't want him calling back to beg. He knew Don had a challenging time keeping people on the payroll.

There was a light knock on the door, and then the delivery men came in with the large leather recliner Jack had picked out. It was a deluxe model with a holder for his glass and remote control. It even had a built-in back massager.

While the delivery men left to retrieve more, Jack tried out the chair and the massager. He closed his eyes again, thinking he'd never get out of the chair. He took in a deep breath to smell the leather. He'd chosen everything in basic black. The saleswoman had tried to convince him to add some color with accent pillows, but he'd dismissed the idea. *I want everything to match my soul.*

It took the men another fifty minutes to get everything inside and set up for him the way he wanted it. He gave both men a ten-dollar tip on their way out since they'd gone to great pains to rearrange the furniture in the bedroom until he was happy with it. He walked through each room admiring his pieces and thinking about how much of the money he'd already spent. Although, it didn't matter because he was going back that night to rob it.

He looked around the living room and into the kitchen, thinking about what kind of décor he would want for his new home. He'd need to purchase his weight-lifting equipment soon, and he decided to buy a computer to put in the second bedroom as well. He wanted to shop online and search for novel and exciting places to rob. *Or maybe I'll start more fires. That was fun too.*

He sat down on the recliner and made a list of all things he wanted to shop for. He'd need to buy new clothes, linens, and a washer and dryer. The first thing, though, was to use his new identity to get a couple of credit cards. Eric promised him that he had a good credit score. He pulled out his wallet and made sure he had two stolen credit cards with him. Before the fun started later that night, he'd do some shopping.

All his life, he had to wear used clothes because his foster families provided new things for their own kids and then handed the old things off to him. The foster parents without children just had more important things to buy, or at least that's what they'd always said. They told him the state didn't give them enough to cover all his needs, so he'd have to do without the luxury of new clothes and toys. He grimaced when he recalled the only new thing he got for Christmas one year from his foster parents at the time—it was a carton of cigarettes. Then, just to show him how nasty the habit was, his foster father made him chain-smoke an entire pack until he puked. After that, Jack had run away. He lived on the streets for a month before the Child Protection Services found him and threw him back into the system.

The more Jack remembered about his life back then, the more pissed off he became. Some of the low-life scumbags were probably still taking in kids and screwing up their lives. Maybe he'd have to put a stop to that. Maybe he'd have to pay them a visit. But not tonight. Tonight, he'd treat himself.

He still had some clothes at the elderly couple's house that he needed to clean out, and he also needed to wipe down everything to remove his prints and DNA, so he drove there first. He didn't feel like doing the cleaning, though, so instead, he burned the house to the ground. The car was the only proof left that he'd been there. He knew a guy, however, who could help with that. Ray Helms was another ex-con he knew, and he worked at a local junkyard. For a hefty price, he'd give Jack a new VIN for the car.

Jack quickly distanced himself from the arson scene and drove to the mall to get his new things.

CHAPTER FORTY-THREE

Rhett proofread the chapter and sent it off to Dave. He was feeling slightly groggy from the Xanax, but it was only 9:00 a.m., so he'd have to power through the morning. He considered going into town for his curtains and paint, but as he looked around the room, he wondered if he should hold off on it. Sarah's warning was, perhaps, affecting him more than he realized. The fire was a tragedy, but it was nonsense to think that the house had deliberately killed them. Still, he was anxious to find out more about the house's history. He checked his email for the third time. Nothing yet.

Sitting there and just waiting was making him stir crazy, so he got up to find something to do. He still didn't want to go shopping, so he decided to work on the repairs. He went outside to fix the floorboards on the back porch. He couldn't avoid glancing at the tombstones first, and he was relieved when he didn't see any ghosts there this time. As he worked on the porch, he wondered if maybe he'd hallucinated the entire thing. He could still be getting over his head injury from the car accident. He pulled his phone out of his pocket to call Dr. Parks at the hospital to see if hallucinations were possible. After speaking with two receptionists, he finally got the doctor on the line.

"Hello, this is Dr. Parks," the man greeted him. "How can I help you?"

"Hi, this is Rhett Shaw. Do you remember me from a couple of days ago? I was in a car wreck and unconscious for a few days."

"Yes, Mr. Shaw, I remember your case. What can I do for you?"

Rhett hesitated before explaining. "Well, I want to know if hallucinations are possible after a head injury like I had."

The doctor quickly asked, "Are you seeing things that aren't there or hearing things?"

Rhett cleared his throat, and his voice was hoarse when he answered. "Well, I think I might have imagined something this morning."

"Hmm. Well, hallucinations can occur after traumatic brain injury. I checked your MRI carefully, though, and it was clear when I released you. However, you may still have symptoms while you finish healing. Also, some medications can cause delusions. I remember the only thing you're on is Xanax, and that shouldn't cause any as long as you take it as prescribed. You're not taking it too often are you?" Dr. Parks asked.

"No, not at all. I took one today after the incident, but otherwise, I haven't taken it since I got home from the hospital," Rhett explained.

"Can you tell me more about what you saw?"

Rhett opened his mouth to explain, but nothing came out. He was too embarrassed to say it aloud. "Umm, I'm sure it was nothing. I write fiction, if you recall, and it was probably just my imagination playing tricks on me."

"Well, if you're seeing things, we'll need to run more tests to make sure you're healing properly. I'm curious about what you think you saw, though," the doctor pressed.

"Um, I-I-I'm fine. S-sorry to bother you," Rhett rushed his words and quickly disconnected the call. He fanned his face, which was no doubt tomato red.

He stood up to go inside to see if the clerk had responded to his email inquiry, but something caught his eye and stopped him. He turned to look at the graves again and saw a silvery image moving around one of them. An icy chill passed over him as he watched the specter dance and shimmer over the grave. It wasn't Sarah this time. This ghost was larger, and he realized it was the spirit of Mrs. Jones. She reached for Rhett and whispered something, but he couldn't hear the words.

"I'm sorry, but what?" he asked, feeling his arm hair standing up.

This time, her voice rang out clearly. She said, "Help us."

Rhett pinched his arm and felt the sting. He wasn't imagining this; she wasn't a hallucination. He spun on his heel and went inside to look up more information on ghosts. Specifically, he wanted to know what made them hold on to the physical plane. He wasn't much of a churchgoer anymore, but he believed in God and heaven, so why weren't the ghosts there? Why hadn't Laura ever visited him if they could move about freely?

He checked his email first, but he still had nothing from the county recorder. He typed his question into the search bar and nervously waited for the results while tapping his fingers on the desk. Numerous articles populated again, and he bypassed those he'd already read. He read through several posts in a chat room, but nothing there was useful. Then he found an interesting blog and read that ghosts will cling to their bodies if they have unfinished business, refuse to accept their death, or cling to a person or object. He read that some are murder victims who stay on earth to see justice done or seek revenge.

Rhett cupped his hands over his face and moaned. How was he supposed to know why the Jones family was roaming the earth? Was it because they were clinging to the house? He supposed he could ask them. Mrs. Jones did ask for his help. *Maybe she wants help, so they can move on to the afterlife.*

He rose from the chair to go outside and talk to her when he noticed his email tab flashing. He clicked on it and saw that the clerk had finally responded. He opened the message with a nervous excitement churning his stomach and read aloud.

"Dear Mr. Shaw, I have the information you requested on 100 Jones Drive in Bondville. The home was built in 1976 and occupied by Richard Jones. When he died in 2001, the house was transferred to his heir, Robert Jones. If you need anything else, simply reply to this message."

Rhett read the message three times while his thoughts churned. If the house was possessed, and not by Robert Jones's family, then it had to be Richard Jones. Sarah had made the house sound evil, and her mother had asked for help, so he had to wonder what Richard did during his life. Was he the evil entity Rhett could feel?

He typed the man's name into the search bar, but the only thing to come up was a list of social media accounts for other men with the same name. If Richard Jones did something awful, there might be a record of it somewhere. He grabbed his keys and drove back to the Bondville Library.

CHAPTER FORTY-FOUR

Rhett entered the library and saw the same scowling librarian as last time. He politely nodded in her direction before going upstairs to the Archives Room. All but one machine was in use, so he quickly sat at the vacant one.

He typed in Richard's name and waited while it performed the search for articles. He found a few stories about men named Richard Jones, but nothing connected them to the house on Jones Drive, so Rhett skipped over them. Then he found what he wanted. There was a lengthy article about several murders and break-ins in Bennington County over a brief period. The police had arrested a primary suspect, Richard Jones, but then the case was dismissed because the chain of custody had been broken, causing the key evidence to be suppressed. Before any additional evidence could be collected for a subsequent arrest, Mr. Jones died from a stroke. He'd been thirty-two at the time of his death.

There was a quote from the chief of police who'd said, "While we didn't have additional evidence for a conviction, we are still looking at Richard Jones for the crimes in question. Since his death, the robberies and associated murders have ceased. I think the citizens of Bennington County can safely assume that it's over."

Rhett stared at the monitor, feeling the hairs on his neck stand up, and his stomach turned. *Richard Jones sounds like Jack. Is that why I've been so inspired since I moved into the house?* His mind was spinning with conclusions.

"Wow, you look like you're reading something interesting," a woman suddenly said, startling Rhett.

He smiled out of shyness at the attractive brunette and replied, "It is interesting."

She smiled back and tried to peek around the machine to see for herself. "Well, my story is boring, so what do you have?"

Rhett was tongue-tied at first. He certainly wasn't going to tell her about the haunted house, so instead, he answered with, "Just something I stumbled on. I didn't find what I was looking for."

"Oh? What are you looking for? Maybe I can help," she offered.

Rhett felt flushed as he tried to produce a good lie. "I was looking up articles about the city's original architecture. I recently moved here, and I'm fascinated with the older buildings in town."

The woman made a sour face. "Are you in construction or an architect?"

Rhett was impressed with her intuition. "I used to be a carpenter. I'm a writer now."

She was about to reply, but someone hissed a loud shushing sound, so she just mouthed, "Oops."

Rhett noticed her glance at his left hand for the second time. She was obviously looking for a wedding ring.

She leaned in and whispered, "Would you like to get a coffee at the café next door? I'll tell you about the town's history. It's my treat."

Rhett knew she was being flirtatious, but he didn't expect her to ask him out. Women were getting bolder he guessed. The shushing sound was made again, so he just nodded in response. *Couldn't hurt. I need to learn to be more sociable again.*

When they reached the bottom of the stairs, she told him, "By the way, I'm Renee."

"It's nice to meet you, Renee. My name is Rhett." He held the library door open for her to exit first.

She giggled. "I thought we were going to be sent to the principal's office for talking."

Rhett grinned at her and said, "Me too. Some people just don't know how to relax." He opened the door to the café and held it for her.

Her cheeks turned a pale pink. "How chivalrous," she mumbled.

He shrugged. "I bet you thought it was dead."

"I did," she answered with a laugh and nodded. "Have you always been that way, or did a woman have to train you?"

He quirked his brow at her. "I suppose my wife trained me." He saw her expression go tight, so he quickly added, "She passed away a few years ago."

"Oh, I'm so sorry," she told him softly. "I lost my husband in a car accident five years ago, so I know what you went through."

"I guess you do," he quietly replied. He pulled her chair out for her and then took the opposite seat. The waitress came by and filled their coffee cups.

"So, tell me about your books," Renee said.

Rhett was glad for the change in topic. He told her about his first two books, but only told her he was working on a third one without giving her details about the plot. He didn't want to think about it after the comparison he'd made between Jack and Richard Jones.

"So, is the new book part three then?" she inquired.

He had to give her something, so he said, "No. It's a crime story."

"Neat. I write some poetry, but it's just for me. I'd never be brave enough to share it, though, and I'd never be able to write a book." She shook her head vigorously.

Rhett shrugged. "You never know until you pick up a pen and try."

She gave him a flirtatious smile. "Well, maybe you can inspire me." He laughed nervously, and it made her turn crimson. "I'm sorry. I'm not usually that forward. The truth is, I've not even dated since I lost Paul, but there was something about you that drew me in. I think it's your kind eyes. They reminded me of him."

Now Rhett was the one with the red face. "Thank you. I've not dated or socialized since I lost my Laura. She was the most important thing in the world to me."

"Do you have kids?"

He shook his head and replied, "No, but we were thinking about it."

Renee sighed, and her eyes dropped to her cup of coffee. "Yeah, so were we." She looked up at him again and forced a shaky smile. "But I've come to realize that life must go on, so here I am." She openly gestured toward him.

Rhett returned her smile and raised his cup in a toast. "Here's to living another day."

They spent the next half hour talking about Bondville, and she made good on her promise to tell him about the town's history. She'd been raised in the quiet community, so she knew quite a bit about it.

Rhett seized the opportunity to find out more about Richard Jones. "Do you remember a string of murders and robberies back around 2001?"

Renee bit her lip and looked off to the side while she thought about it. "You know, I think I might remember something. I was sixteen back then, and I can remember my parents being paranoid about something. They insisted that I always come straight home from school, they installed new deadbolts on the doors, and they even put in an alarm system. Why?"

He quickly thought about his answer before saying anything. In the brief time they spent talking, he decided he wouldn't mind seeing her again, which meant that she'd probably be at his house in the future. Thus, he couldn't avoid telling her the truth—except for the part about the ghosts.

"Well, the article I was reading when you interrupted me"—he winked—"was about the primary suspect in that case. He died in his house before being convicted, though, and that's where I currently live. I was researching the home's history."

She raised a brow at him and teased, "Oh, so you lied to me then?"

Rhett opened his arms with a shrug. "Busted."

"It's okay, but that's creepy about the guy dying there—especially if he was the criminal they were after. I wonder if he ever killed someone in your house. Do you think so?" Her eyes were wide with excitement, and she made a lot of gestures.

The lines in Rhett's forehead deepened. "I don't know. The article didn't say anything like that. It just said he'd been arrested for the crimes. There weren't any specific details."

"I see," she murmured and looked at her watch. "I hate to leave in the middle of our conversation, but I'm due at the eye doctor in fifteen minutes, so I need to get going."

"Okay, I'll walk you out." Rhett threw money onto the table to cover the coffee and tip.

"Hey, I said it was my treat," Renee protested with her wallet in hand.

He gave her a lazy grin. "You can get the next one."

She crinkled her nose and told him, "Will do." Then she wrote her phone number on a napkin and passed it to him. "Call me, okay?"

He nodded and stood to get the door for her. "I will. I promise." He walked her to her yellow Mustang and then waved as she drove away. Whistling to himself, he went back to his truck in the library parking lot.

Maybe I'm ready to get back out there after all.

CHAPTER FORTY-FIVE

Rhett thought about his chat with Renee during the drive home. Given the grief he still felt over losing Laura, he was surprised to find himself taken with the woman. Renee was certainly pretty, but he hadn't considered the idea of dating again, and he wasn't sure he was ready. He decided, though, it couldn't hurt to make a new friend. The fact that she'd also lost a spouse gave them a connection he wouldn't find with most women.

He pulled into the driveway and then sat still, looking up at the house. Instead of working on repairs, he decided to do more research on Richard Jones. There had to be something online that he hadn't seen earlier. He wanted to learn everything he could about the man and the crimes he had been accused of. Somewhere inside that information were the answers he wanted about the house. He went inside, grabbed a beer, and sat down to start his research.

Instead of searching by Richard's name again, he searched for information on the crime spree in 2001. He found news coverage on the crimes that he'd not seen earlier. Richard was mentioned in a couple of those stories, which made him wonder if he'd passed over it earlier or if it hadn't shown up. He grabbed his pen and notepad and jotted some of the information down. He noted businesses and neighborhoods that had been robbed and where people were killed. When he finished writing the last detail, he got up and paced the room, nervously clenching his fists and grinding his teeth. The man was so much like Jack.

"Are you communicating with me through my book?" he asked aloud and continued his pacing.

In response, a clock chimed upstairs. The problem was his clocks didn't chime. He looked at his watch and saw that it was 1:00 p.m., whereas the clock rang nine times.

"Are you trying to drive me mad?"

He punched the wall and regretted it as pain radiated up the length of his arm. He heard a low, menacing moan as he rubbed at the stinging in his elbow. He took it as a warning from the house.

Rhett dosed himself with another Xanax and a couple of aspirin for the pain and sat back down at his computer. He opened his book to the next page, but it was futile; he couldn't possibly concentrate enough to write. Instead, he re-read the details of the heinous crimes. He knew that what he read wasn't the entire story, though. The police were probably holding back some key details just in case Richard wasn't the perpetrator. So, if he wanted to learn more, he needed to go to the source.

He grabbed his keys and drove to the police station. He'd just tell them that it was research for his book.

CHAPTER FORTY-SIX

Rhett explained to the receptionist at the Bondville Police Department that he wanted to speak to someone about an old case involving homicide and robberies. Then he took a seat in the waiting area while she fetched someone to help him. He had never had any trouble with the law, but it still made him nervous to be there. Soon after he sat down, the door to the main room swung open, and a tall man in a suit jacket greeted him.

"I'm Detective Mulford with the Homicide Unit. Jane tells me you have questions about an old case, so how can I help you?" the man asked without extending his hand.

Rhett stood and initiated a handshake. "I'm Rhett Shaw, and I have some questions regarding a case back in 2001."

"Oh"—the man rubbed his chin—"well, that dates before my time, so let me grab Detective Hulsey. He's been here the longest and may remember something from back then. I warn you, though, that certain facts can only be revealed in solved cases." He shot Rhett a questioning glance.

Rhett nodded once. "I understand, and I've read the released details about the case. It was believed to be solved at the time, but then evidence was suppressed."

The detective grimaced. "Yeah, that happens sometimes. Walk this way, and I'll take you to Detective Hulsey."

Rhett looked around the busy room as he followed the detective. Several heads looked up to see who was walking in, and he supposed that was probably more for safety reasons than curiosity. He hoped they didn't think he was a suspect being questioned. Detective Mulford stopped at the desk of a large man with a head of thick red hair and a beard to match. He explained to the other detective that Rhett had questions.

"It's an oldie," he said before walking off.

Detective Hulsey gestured to the chair in front of his desk. "Have a seat." He closed the file folder he had been looking at and set it aside. "What is the case you're interested in?"

Rhett nervously wrung his hands in his lap and replied, "I would like to ask you questions about a string of murders and robberies back in 2001. The police thought Richard Jones was responsible and arrested him, but the evidence was inadmissible." He knew he'd rushed his words, but the detective appeared to be following along.

Detective Hulsey jotted a note on his legal pad and then typed something into his computer. "Are you a reporter?" he inquired.

"Oh, no, I'm an author. I think I want to write a book about the case, and I just need more information than what I found online and at the library."

Detective Hulsey sighed. "I see. Well, you already know that we pegged Richard Jones as the doer, so what kind of questions do you have that you haven't already found the answers to?"

Rhett wasn't prepared to answer that question. He hadn't planned this out enough. He took a deep breath and asked, "Well, for starters, can you tell me about the evidence that was thrown out?" He watched while the detective typed again on his keyboard.

"Let's see. We had fingerprints and DNA, but the chain of custody was broken, and you know what happened after that."

Rhett followed up with another question. "Was he already in the system, and you matched his prints, or did you have reason to suspect him?"

Detective Hulsey sighed again and leaned back in his chair, causing it to groan under his weight. "According to the system, he didn't have any priors, so we must've had other reasons, but I can't remember that far back. We'd have to go back to the handwritten notes in the file, and a case dating sixteen years ago is in the archives. I'll tell you, though, no one is going to offer to dig for it unless new information came to light, and we had to reopen the case. It's a mess down there."

Rhett casually nodded and folded his hands. "I understand, and that's fine. How many counts of homicide was he facing?"

The detective referred back to his computer screen. "We pegged him for nine counts of theft and four counts of homicide."

Rhett's eyes opened wide. "And yet the judge dismissed the case on a technicality. Unbelievable."

Detective Hulsey nodded in agreement. "Unfortunately, that kind of thing happens more often than you'd think. The judge's hands were tied by the law."

"I bet that pisses you guys off," Rhett remarked while gesturing to the room.

"Absolutely! You think you've solved a case, and then some asshole fucks up, and all your hard work is out the window, and you have to start from scratch. Only then, they know you're on to them, so they're more careful." He stopped talking long enough to take a sip of coffee. "Of course, in Jones's case, he died before we could find anything else on him, but the crime wave ceased, so we considered the case closed based on the initial evidence."

Rhett tried to think like Rodney Small. What questions would he ask in this situation? "Did you ever recover any of the stolen property? After he died, did you search his house?"

The detective looked at him like he was offended. "Yeah, of course we did. We didn't find anything, though. He probably sold everything, but we checked with the local pawn shops, and nothing turned up for us on that. Now, let me ask you something. Why this case? What about it makes you want to write the story?"

Rhett felt choked for words as he tried to think up a viable explanation. "I just moved here from Brooklyn, and I saw the house. It interested me as possibly being a fixer-upper, and then someone told me what happened there."

The detective's desk phone rang then, and he promptly answered it, holding one finger up to Rhett. When he finished the call, he grabbed the file folder he'd closed earlier and rose from his chair.

"I have an active case with a new lead, so I have to cut this short. Anything else you need, you'll have to find in public records." He pointed toward the exit sign. "That's the way back out."

Rhett took his cue and left the station. He hadn't learned anything useful, so that meant he'd have to hunt for the rest of the answers. The best place to start was the house.

CHAPTER FORTY-SEVEN

When Rhett reached home, he found his flashlight and a paperclip and then climbed the ladder into the attic. He wanted to look inside the locked trunk and all around the area for clues.

After bending it straight, he used the paperclip to pick the padlock on the trunk. He'd learned how to do it several years ago when Laura had lost the key to the lock on their storage shed.

He made quick work of the padlock and opened the dusty lid, cringing at the high-pitched creaking sound it made. He shined the light inside and cleared away numerous cobwebs to see the contents. He waded through loose photos, books, cassette tapes, a bound stack of letters with Diane Carter as the addressee, and a stack of journals with the name Diane Jones neatly written on the outside. He set those aside along with the letters and put everything else back inside the trunk.

He walked around the small area looking for anything else he might find useful. He came across old lamps, baby clothes, dresses, and a rocking horse. He even found an old Boy Scout badge collection, no doubt belonging to Robert, but he didn't find any clues. He exited the attic with the stack of letters and the journals tucked under his arm.

Sitting at his desk, he started with the letters. They were from Robert to Diane when they were courting. Rhett felt embarrassed by the private content, so he bound them back together and set them off to the side. He sorted the journals by the dates written on the outside and then opened the first one dated 2001. He skimmed the pages for anything connected to the house or Richard Jones and finally found a reference to the crimes. According to her entry, she and Robert had just gotten married when the spree began. He was working overtime, which left her home alone, and she was scared. She mentioned the people who'd been murdered and the places that were robbed.

Rhett sympathized with her and what she had gone through. He recalled Laura's anxiety when he'd had to leave her alone a couple of times in the city, and that was just with the normal crime rate—not a maniac killer on the loose. A deep chill settled in his chest when he read what she'd written about one of the murders.

"One of the victims was missing her hands, and I found out from a friend at the police station that they were taken postmortem. What kind of monster does something like that? I wish they'd catch the maniac, so we can have peace of mind again. I hate that Rob is always working and leaving me alone in the country. It's scary enough out here without a murderer on the loose."

Detective Hulsey didn't mention the missing hands earlier when they spoke. Rhett didn't think it was something that could be forgotten either, so why hold back on the information? It must've become public knowledge after Richard's death.

He shivered one more time and then continued reading. He read through her repeated concerns about the crimes, but then her tone changed as she talked about discovering her pregnancy. The rest of the journal was focused on the milestones and how she was feeling right up to the birth of Patrick.

The next journal began with more notes about the baby, so Rhett skimmed over those parts until he found a mention of Richard.

"Uncle Richard was arrested today for the crime wave. He's being charged for the thefts and murders, and I just can't believe it. He is a kind man, so I know they have the wrong person! He has been so helpful to us as we start our lives together, and I refuse to believe that Rob is related to the evil monster destroying our once peaceful community."

Rhett could almost hear her saying the words. He could hear the fear she felt and the love for her uncle-in-law. Her tone changed a few pages later, though.

"The lawyer explained the evidence collected against Uncle Richard. He said they claim to have matching DNA and prints. I don't know what to do with that information. How do I process proof that our beloved relative is a cold-blooded murderer? Rob quit the overtime hours to be home more with me and Patrick while we deal with this. I'm not going to the jailhouse to see Richard. I can't look at him, so Rob will have to go alone if he even wants to. Thankfully, the break-ins and murders have stopped."

In a later entry, she talked about the case being dismissed.

"The judge threw the case out today. Richard's attorney says it's because of a problem with the evidence, but I found out on my own that the chain of custody had been broken. That doesn't mean anything was tampered with. It doesn't mean he's innocent, and I'm worried now that he's out. Rob installed a second deadbolt on the doors today to make me feel better, but how can I? I won't even let Patrick sleep in the nursery while this goes on. He has to sleep next to me."

Rhett felt bad for the woman. He could only imagine the terror and disappointment she must've felt. He took a break long enough to make a fresh pot of industrial-strength coffee. He was feeling tired from the Xanax he'd taken in the morning, but he wanted to keep reading. He looked out the kitchen window toward the graves, but he didn't see anything this time. When the coffee finished brewing, he filled his largest mug and went back to reading the journals. He skimmed over random notations until he came across more information about Richard.

"It's been three days since Richard's release, and thankfully, he hasn't tried to contact us. We have nothing supportive to say to him."

Rhett took a brief pause to wonder what he'd do in that situation. Would he be able to stand by a relative or friend while knowing they were guilty? That would be a difficult decision for some. Personally, he didn't think he could. He rubbed his temples and eyes as he felt a tension headache coming on and grabbed two more aspirin from his desk drawer. The coffee was too hot to drink yet, so he chewed the aspirin instead, leaving a bitter taste in his mouth until he could wash it away. He turned the page in the journal to continue reading. Her next entry talked about Richard's death.

"Richard was found dead in his home today by his lawyer after he failed to show up for their appointment. I feel bad to admit this, but I'm relieved. The police reassured us that he was the one they were after. Rob is taking things pretty hard, but I'm just glad it can finally be over. I hate going out in public because people know we're related to him. They stare at us with accusing eyes. I don't want my child to have to grow up with family shame. I'm trying to convince Rob to move away from here, but he's being stubborn. He thinks we can handle it, but I don't think I'm strong enough."

Rhett skipped over some non-related entries and a comment that the funeral was held, but they didn't attend it. Then he found the first mention of the house.

"Rob saw our lawyer today. For some reason, Richard left everything to him including his house. I told Rob I still want to move away, but he says we can't afford it. He wants to move into the house and get rid of our mortgage payments. I told him that I didn't want to live in a house that was paid for with dirty money, and we had our first fight since Patrick's birth. He insists we move there, and I'm not going to leave him, so my hands are tied."

Wow. She had a bad feeling about the house before she moved into it. Rhett wondered if it was just because of Richard's dirty deeds, or if she'd always disliked it. He read over her notes about the move and decorating the house to get rid of the evidence linking Richard to it. They sold off his belongings at a public auction and used the money to remodel the house. She commented that it was sick individuals who got off on pain that came to the auction. They thought it was neat to have something that once belonged to an alleged serial killer. Rhett couldn't deny that humans are fascinated with the morbid. That's why he was writing crime fiction now. Stories about serial killers are difficult to ignore.

Thinking about his book, he decided to write for a few minutes. He'd received another demanding email from Dave earlier in the morning, which he'd skipped over, but he couldn't put it off any longer. He needed to produce. He'd write one chapter and then go back to reading Diane's journals.

CHAPTER FORTY-EIGHT

Jack returned home with several shopping bags full of new clothes and a new laptop computer. He laughed to himself when he recalled the cashier's expression as she rang up his clothing. She took one look at him standing in line wearing his tattered shirt and stained jeans and probably thought he couldn't afford to buy a pair of boxers in that store let alone shirts or pants. Well, he showed her. His total came to $680—he treated himself to name brands—and he paid with one of the stolen Visa cards. Every use of the cards was a gamble, and he held his breath until the receipt printed out. Credit card roulette was a risky business—he never knew if the owner called it in as stolen and closed the account or if it was maxed out from him using it too often. Therefore, he rotated them out regularly. Today, he was using the elderly man's card. He doubted the bodies had been discovered yet, so he had a few days to use them. After he set up his laptop, though, he was going to get one to match his new identity— Damon Bradshaw needed spending power. *Hell, I might even be able to pay the bill a couple of times.* He glanced at his watch. It was almost time to go out for the night.

He heated up a TV dinner and ate while he set up his laptop. He'd visited the library numerous times before to learn how to navigate the internet, so he knew enough to get started once the computer was up and running. He needed to have service installed first, so he pulled out his phone and looked up the nearest provider. He gave them a quick call and scheduled his appointment for 10:00 a.m. to have both satellite and internet access installed. He customized his start screen and settings, following the instructions step by step. When he was finished, he played solitaire until it was time to go to the furniture store, which had been closed for over an hour already.

GET
OUT

Jack pulled up to the alley behind the furniture store and found a single car parked in the rear lot. He figured it belonged to the store manager, who was probably still closing the books and locking up. That would make things easier for Jack because he wouldn't have to attempt to disable the alarm system, so he just waited for the man to exit the building. He didn't have to wait long either. The short man he'd seen earlier in the day waddled out the back door, turned his key in the lock, and then proceeded to his car. Jack was quick, though, and he was waiting on the other side of it, which was in the man's blind spot. As soon as the manager came into view, Jack lunged and brought him to the ground. He quickly pistol-whipped him in the head several times. The butt of the gun came down with blinding force, and blood spewed all over the pavement as a loud crunch rang out. He left the man lying there, not knowing or caring if he was dead or alive. If he were to wager a bet, though, he'd bet the manager was dead. He retrieved the blue bank bag the man had dropped and took off running toward his car.

Jack pulled off the sweltering ski mask and sped down the highway toward home. When he reached his condo, he threw his blood-stained clothes into his new washer along with a cup full of bleach.

It's a good thing I wore my old clothes.

He sat on the couch and counted the money from the bank bag. There was $7,579 in cash. Almost $4,000 of it had come from him. The rest of the contents were checks, which he couldn't do anything with, so he ripped them up and threw them in the trash, immediately taking it to the Dumpster. When he returned, he looked around the room at his free elegant furniture and laughed to himself.

CHAPTER FORTY-NINE

Rhett poured himself another mug of coffee after sending the chapter to Dave. Then he opened Diane's journal up to where he'd left off. His eyes went wide as he read the next entry.

"There's something odd about this house. It's as if I can feel Richard's residual energy here. I swear I can feel him watching me. Rob thinks it's all in my head, but it's too real to just be my imagination. There's something ominous about this house. I hear weird noises, such as doors slamming or a clock chiming, all the time. I can tell the baby hears them too because it makes him start fussing. I want to move away from here and this whole town. Everywhere I go, people stare. I feel like we'll never escape the shame Richard has bestowed on our family."

Rhett leaned back in his chair and digested her words. She'd heard the same things he's been hearing, which made him think it must be Richard's restless spirit lingering in the house. He wondered why Sarah hadn't said anything about her great-uncle. She'd only said the *house* gets angry. He would ask her about Richard the next time he saw her. He went on to the next entry in the neatly printed journal. It was dated three days later.

"I still feel like something is wrong with this house. I'm always cold. I set the AC to 75 degrees, but I'm still chilly. Sometimes, too, when I glance at the mirror, I see someone standing there with me. When I turn around, though, I'm alone. Rob still dismisses my concerns. He's changed since we moved in, and I don't feel like we're connecting as much as we used to. He went back on overtime to afford my car repairs. I hate that Patrick and I are stuck in the house, but without a second running car, we can't go anywhere. Maybe I should go back to work, but I hate the idea of leaving the baby with a sitter. I talked with my mom today, and she agreed with Rob. She said I've always had an active imagination. I might see a therapist when the car is fixed."

Rhett related to the woman's frustrations. He couldn't help but find it comforting, though, to know he wasn't the only one who'd heard things and seen things. "It's nice to know I'm not totally insane," he assured himself aloud.

He glanced down at the journal and skimmed over the next couple of entries. They were mostly about her son or the kind of day she was having and didn't mention anything about the house. The third one, however, did.

"I heard a woman's screams today. Patrick and I were playing in the living room when we heard it coming from upstairs. The baby looked up and began crying, so I know he heard it too. It was the sound of someone in agony. I have to wonder if someone besides Richard died in this house."

Rhett wondered that now too. Did Richard murder someone inside the house, and what happened to the one woman's hands? Maybe it isn't Richard haunting the place. Maybe it's one of his victims. Diane could've figured it out, so he needed to keep reading. However, his eyes were feeling strained, so he marked his place in the journal and decided to go for a walk around the yard.

The sun was setting, and the temperature had cooled off to the mid-sixties already. It was supposed to be mostly sunny and close to 73 degrees over the next five days. Since it was late in May, he felt it was safe to put in the flowerbeds. He felt the need to plant something that would make him feel closer to Laura, so he'd plant her favorite flowers, which were daisies and petunias. He looked up at the house, which was cast in shadows, and grimaced. He really should paint the outside and repair the roof first, so he decided to start painting in the morning.

He walked around the backyard and listened to the wildlife in the woods. He heard a hoot from an owl and the scurrying of small animals among the bushes as they tried to hide from the predator. It was peaceful until a shrill scream from inside the house pierced the air. Rhett spun around while his heart tried to beat straight out of his chest. The sound was exactly like Diane had said—someone was in agony. It was the bone-chilling cry of death.

"You heard it too, didn't you?" a soft voice asked from behind him.

Rhett recognized Sarah's voice and turned to see her glowing transparency hovering over her grave again. "The scream? Yes, I heard it too. Who is it?" he gently probed.

He could make out a shrug from the ghostly child. "I don't know. I've never known who she is. She doesn't come out here, but sometimes I can see her in the window."

Rhett squeezed his eyes shut and rubbed his hand across them. The sudden pounding inside his head was relentless. "Could it be your mother?" he wondered.

The ghost shook her head. "No, she doesn't ever go inside the house. She stays here and cries since we aren't in heaven."

He felt his heartbreaking for the family, and he felt his eyes sting as he fought back tears of his own. "Do you know about your father's uncle?" he choked out.

Sarah shook her head full of long curls and opened her mouth to say something, but then she turned her back to him. "I have to go now," she called over her shoulder and vanished into the ground while he watched.

CHAPTER FIFTY

When Rhett stepped inside the house, he heard the invisible clock chime nine strokes. He knew it wasn't that late, but he looked at his watch out of habit—it was only 7:10. *What is that all about?* His brain was hurting from the madness, and the fierce pounding was only getting worse. He took three aspirin this time and a Xanax to top it off. He reached for the journal but then hesitated. He felt too lousy to read. He opted, instead, for a hot shower.

After the relaxing wash, Rhett sat down at his laptop again, trying to decide if he wanted to write more or read more. His headache was finally easing up, so he decided to start reading and go from there. He read a few entries about milestones the baby was reaching with only repeated comments about the house. She'd mentioned more about feeling cold, items being misplaced, and hearing the clock. His eyelids started to feel heavy not long into the reading, so he decided to call it quits and go to bed.

He woke up around midnight and searched the darkness. He felt like he wasn't alone in the room. He had the closet light on, since the house was still new to him, and when he strained his eyes, he could see movement in the shadows. He bolted upright in his bed.

"Who's there?" he called out, but he was met with silence.

It didn't feel like his encounters with Sarah or Diane Jones. It felt like a malevolent presence was hanging over the room, and it caused a freezing chill to pass right through his chest, choking off his breathing. He considered sleeping on the couch again, but then he talked himself out of it.

"Damn it!" he cursed aloud to whoever would listen, "This is *my* house now. Let me live in peace."

He started to close his eyes, but an ear-piercing scream made him jump out of his skin. He groaned and put the extra pillow over his ears and went back to sleep, refusing to be driven from the house by the restless spirits hanging around. When he woke up the second time, slivers of white light were streaming in through the tattered window shade, which still needed replacing. He walked through his usual morning routine before heading downstairs to start the coffee. He stepped onto the back porch and took several deep breaths of the clean air. It was so refreshing to be away from the filthy city—even if he had ghost problems. He glanced toward the four grave plots and saw Diane's spirit hovering around her tombstone.

"Help us," she called out to him. "Please, will you help us?"

He descended the three steps to the yard and approached the silvery silhouette. "Help you with what? How can I help you?"

He saw her glance up at the house. "Help us escape, so we can move on," she pleaded.

Rhett didn't know what to say except, "How? What can I possibly do?"

She looked at the house again. Only this time, she looked frightened by what she saw. "You have to help her first," she replied in a whisper before sinking back into her grave.

After the odd exchange, Rhett looked over his shoulder at the house to see if he could see whatever had distressed her, but everything looked normal. He shook it off and went back inside to get his coffee and start writing or reading. When he poured the liquid into his mug, though, he noticed the lack of steam. He felt the outside of the mug, and it was cool to the touch.

He groaned aloud, "Oh, come on! Don't fuck with my caffeine!" With another grunt, he put the mug inside the microwave and heated it up.

With hot coffee in hand now, he was ready to do something productive. After his laptop came to life, he checked his email account first. Of course, he had a message from Dave, demanding even more progress on the book. He claimed, in his own way, that Rhett wasn't working up to his potential. While Rhett typed out a reply, he had to grind his teeth to control his temper. He explained that he had a lot on his mind and several repairs on the house that were demanding his focus. He did promise, however, that he would try to churn out two chapters or more by the end of the day.

He also had an email from Bridget. She wanted to know if he'd changed his mind about her coming to visit while she was in town that weekend. He sent a short reply, simply stating that he hadn't. She made him think about Renee, though. He dug out the napkin with her number neatly printed on it from his desk drawer and set it aside for later. He still wanted to talk more with her; he just didn't know if he had the nerve to date her, or anyone else for that matter. He wasn't sure if he were ready to swim in the dating pool again, but it couldn't hurt to get his feet wet. His therapist would be proud of him for taking that step. That was until he found out Rhett talked to ghosts; then he would, without a doubt, confine him to a padded room.

Rhett picked up Diane's journal and opened it to where he'd left off. Her next entry spoke more about Richard's crimes. Specifically, she talked about the murders.

"The police came back to the house to search again for anything tying Richard to the crimes. They said they were looking for stolen goods and Ellie Morrison's hands. They said her family and the families of the other victims wanted closure. Rob was at work, and I didn't like being alone in the house with the two detectives. They ransacked every room, trying to find anything to prove their case once and for all. They even tore into my flowerbeds to make sure nothing was buried there. They didn't find anything, though, so I asked what that meant for the case. One detective told me, 'It means that he probably sold everything or has more property somewhere else, and it's stashed there.' I asked if maybe they had the wrong man, and he said, 'I don't think so, but time will tell.' As soon as they drove away, I heard the screams again. The house is mocking me."

Rhett closed the journal again, paced the living room a few times, and then decided to work on the basement. His nerves were on edge, so he needed something constructive to do with his clenching hands. He also needed to throw in a load of laundry while he was down there.

He'd bought materials to install more shelving, so he'd have a nice work area. He was considering building custom cabinets to sell. Over the past couple of weeks, he'd reconnected with the carpenter side of himself, and it felt good.

Whistling a cheerful tune, he put the skeleton key in his pocket, grabbed his tool belt, materials, and dirty clothes, and made his way into the basement. He thought he heard whispering in its shadowy depths, but he didn't run away. He was going to take back his house.

CHAPTER FIFTY-ONE

Rhett threw his clothes into the washer and put up one set of shelves before quitting because his hands were aching from drilling into the basement walls. He flexed his fingers wide to ease the cramping, but it didn't help with the burning ache. The noise had brought his headache back with full force also, so he climbed the stairs and went for the aspirin. He decided if the headache pain kept up for much longer, he'd need to schedule an appointment with a local doctor. It's not a problem he'd had before, and it could be related to his head injury, so he wouldn't put it off much longer just in case.

It was quickly warming up outside, so he wanted to get some painting completed. He painted the front porch brick red and the window shutters to match. Then he did the same to the rear porch and shutters. The yard was empty today, which made it eerily quiet while he worked.

He fetched his ladder and the power washer he'd purchased to get grime and peeled paint washed off the wood clapboard siding. He'd have to give it a day or two to dry before he could apply a new coat of paint and replace any bad boards.

He was careful to avoid the wet porch while he washed the rest of the house. When he finished, he stepped back to admire it, and it looked a lot brighter now that it was grime-free. He'd probably need to put two coats of paint on it, but it would be worth his time.

A cool breeze suddenly blew past and made him spin around as the hairs on his neck stood up. He was no longer alone in the yard.

"Can you help us?" Diane Jones asked again.

Rhett saw the pleading in her eyes, and it tugged at his heart. "I've been reading your journals," he told her. "Are there answers in them?"

She looked up at the house before telling him, "I think so. I wasn't able to help her, though, and she punished us." Before he could ask to whom she was referring, she vanished into her grave.

He cleaned up his paintbrush mess and put the tools back inside before sitting down to read some more of Diane's past. He needed to find out whom she was talking about, so he also turned the computer back on and ran more searches on the crimes Richard had allegedly committed. He wanted to specifically know who his murder victims were. After digging through articles for an hour, he compiled a list of names. Then he grabbed his keys and drove back to the police station to talk to Detective Hulsey again.

CHAPTER FIFTY-TWO

Detective Hulsey didn't appear too thrilled to see Rhett again. "I told you all I can, Mr. Shaw. Like I said, you'll have to dig through public information for anything else."

Rhett sat down in the chair across from the man anyway. "I just have a couple of follow-up questions, and then I'll get out of your hair."

The detective laced his fingers together and placed his hands on his desk. "Like what?"

Rhett pulled the neatly folded sheet of paper out of his pocket and placed it in front of the other man. "Here are the names of the murder victims. I read that the woman missing her hands was Ellie Morrison. She was his fourth and final murder victim, at least that you know of, right?"

Detective Hulsey looked down and off to the side while he searched his memory. "Yeah, she was. I can still see her face too. Her eyes were wide open in terror."

Rhett didn't want the haunting image to be part of his memory too, so he tried to replace it with something else. The refurbished house popped into his mind.

"It's something I don't think I can ever forget even if I want to, you know?" the detective continued.

Rhett nodded in understanding. "I can imagine. Do you think he killed anyone inside the house?"

"Well, we never found forensic evidence to prove that theory, so no, I don't think so."

Rhett mulled that over for his next question. "So, no bodies were recovered on his property then, but you never found her hands, right?"

Detective Hulsey looked disgusted when he nodded in affirmation. "Yeah, that's right."

"Why do you suppose he took her hands? Did he take anything from the other three victims?" Rhett wondered.

"I'm not sure, but I think I can recall a close friend of hers mentioning diamond rings. Maybe he couldn't get the rings off her fingers. It could be, though, that he wanted a trophy of some kind. He didn't take body parts from the others, however, so that's probably not the reason unless he was escalating." He leaned back in his chair and studied Rhett's expression. "Are you sure you want to open up this can of worms? You'll be bringing up some painful memories for people."

Rhett shrugged and told the man, "People don't forget their loved ones or tragedies. They just choose to move past them. Besides, I'm too wrapped up in the story to back out now."

Before the detective could respond, another man stopped at his desk and asked him about the case from the previous night.

"I was looking at it, but I got interrupted. I'll let you know when I see something," Detective Hulsey replied.

When the other man walked away, Rhett asked, "What happened last night?"

At first, it didn't look like the detective was going to tell him, but then he said, "It's been on the news already, so I can tell you. Another store in town was robbed, and the closing manager was killed."

Rhett thought back to his last chapter about Jack. The similarity was already eerie. "How was he killed?"

Detective Hulsey cocked his head. "That I can't disclose."

"Because anyone could step forward and say they did it, right?"

The detective tapped his temple. "Right. You might want to write about all the shit going on in the past few weeks if you're looking for a story. This is normally a well-behaved community, but something's changed lately. There hasn't been this much criminal activity since, well, since Richard Jones."

Rhett slowly nodded and rose from the chair. "Yeah, I'll think about it. I'm going to get out of your hair now, so you can get back to your case. Thanks for the information."

The detective replied with a single nod and then opened his files up on his desk to get to work on the recent crimes.

Rhett felt like his air supply was being cut off, and he had to get out of there. He certainly couldn't confess that he was writing about the recent crimes before they happened. Or was he writing about them after they happened but before they were public knowledge? Either way, it was bad juju, and he somehow felt responsible. But was it him or just the house?

He decided he wanted professional help, but it wasn't the psychiatrist of whom he was thinking. He sat inside the truck in the police department parking lot and ran a search on his phone for metaphysical shops in Vermont. He found two shops in the state, and one, which was named After Dark, was only thirty-three miles away. Rhett typed the address into the truck's GPS and began the drive.

CHAPTER FIFTY-THREE

Rhett entered the mysterious shop, causing bells over the door to chime. A young woman with short red hair looked up from the book she was reading, and a customer looked over her shoulder from the shelf she was perusing. He suddenly felt tongue-tied when the cashier waited for him to say something.

She finally broke the silence by popping her bubble gum and asking, "Can I help you find something, sweetie?" She put one hand on her hip and gave him a look of impatience.

Feeling self-conscious, he whispered his answer, so the other customer wouldn't hear him. "I'm looking for anything that will help me with a paranormal problem I'm having." She raised her brow to question him. "Ghosts," he whispered.

"You need help with ghosts?" Her voice was loud and carried through the store.

So much for being incognito. He jerked his head up and down while his eyes darted over to the customer. She wasn't paying him any attention though. The redhead popped her gum again and motioned for him to follow her into the next room.

"In here, we have things that will help to communicate with spirits or banish them, so which is it for you?"

He grinned sheepishly. "I am already communicating with them. I—"

"Them?" she interrupted with a little smile.

"Yes, there is a family and then an I-don't know-what kind of ghost."

She bit her lower lip and looked over her shoulder at a closed door. "Let me get Rosa. She is more knowledgeable about ghosts than I am." She didn't wait for his okay before walking off.

He walked around the interesting room and looked at the plethora of paraphernalia spread out. He saw sections labeled "witchcraft, ghosts, and shape-shifters." There was even a small area marked off for black magic. There were candles, herbs, animal bones, decks of tarot cards, crystals, books, charms, and so much more.

He jumped when a door suddenly swung open. A petite woman, who appeared to be in her fifties, exited along with the redhead.

"Chandra tells me you have questions about ghosts. My name is Rosa, and I can help you," she announced with a thick Italian accent.

Rhett gave her a weak smile and tucked his hands inside his pockets. He felt odd there. He felt judged. "I do have questions about ghosts, that's correct."

She tilted her head in the direction of the area marked off for ghosts and began to walk toward it. He hesitantly followed. "I can tell you're nervous to be here. You aren't sure if you believe in what you see, am I right?"

He sighed and looked at his feet. "In the beginning, I thought it was stress and a lack of sleep, but now, I know what I've seen and heard are real. I just don't know what to do with them."

She smiled kindly at him to put him at ease. "Well, you've come to the right place for help. Chandra mentioned that you have more than one specter. Is that right?"

"Yes, that's also correct. You see, there was a fire six years ago, and it killed the family of four living in the house. The daughter was the first to show herself and talk to me, and then her mother has also done so a couple of times. I've not seen the father or son yet."

Her eyes were wide with interest. "I see. Are they friendly then, and where do you see them?"

"Yes, they're friendly enough. I see them at their graves in the yard. The girl warned me about the house, though, and the mother asked me to help them move on."

She nodded slowly with comprehension. "They've lost their path into the light, which is why they aren't moving on, but what is that about the house?"

Rhett spent the next several minutes explaining the house's history. He described the strange noises and things he's seen, and he told her about Diane's journals. He watched her expression grow more curious as he described everything.

When he finished, she said, "That's all very interesting indeed." She held up one finger to her mouth while she sought the answers in her mind's eye. "I think either someone was killed in the house, or the man you spoke of is refusing to leave his earthly possessions. However, you said the spirit mentioned 'she' punished them, so it's probably the first theory. Of course, that would make her a vengeful spirit if she burned them up in the house, so getting her to leave will pose a challenge. As for the family, you should be able to help them leave by calling upon their religious beliefs. Summon the Archangels to show the white light to them again and guide them into it."

Rhett furrowed his brow and crossed his arms over his chest. "Okay, that sounds fairly simple. What about the other one, though? She's the one in the house, and she's driving me crazy with her pranks and the noises."

She smiled kindly again and patted his arm. "Don't worry too much. Ghosts don't usually cause physical harm to humans, and there are a couple of things to try." She grabbed a book from the shelf and handed it to him. "This will help guide you. You'll need white sage to help you cleanse, which I sell. Also, you can get holy water from any Catholic church and use that. Not one thing always works, so you may have to try a few things."

"Anything else I should do?"

"Yes, keep working on the house. You said the house seems to like it, which means the spirit within the house likes it. Also, you shouldn't try to contact her. Don't try to summon her for a talk."

Rhett grimaced. "I really hadn't thought about that, but why not? It would be easier if she could tell me what she wants."

She laughed lightly. "It's not that simple. If you don't know what you're doing when contacting a spirit, you could open a portal that shouldn't be opened. A chain of events could be set in motion that would keep that spirit grounded forever and possibly invite more in."

He shook his head. "I certainly don't want that."

"Start with the book and the sage. Then you can always call or come back if nothing works."

Rhett thanked Rosa for the information and went to the cashier.

Chandra smiled knowingly and rang up his items. "Please visit us again," she said, handing him his shopping bag. "We are always here to help."

"Thank you," Rhett replied, "I might need to take you up on that."

He wasted no time in leaving the peculiar store and driving home. He was anxious to try out suggestions from the book.

CHAPTER FIFTY-FOUR

Rhett made it home forty-five tension-filled minutes later. He immediately sat down at his desk and opened the new book to the table of contents.

It had sections on explaining ghosts and why they don't move on, how to communicate with them, how to nicely demand that they leave, what to do if that doesn't work, who to ask for help, and famous haunted locations throughout the world. Rhett skipped to the section on demanding that they leave. He read that you are supposed to ask nicely, yet firmly, for them to leave your home. You have to go about it in a non-confrontational way, or they might turn into an even bigger pest.

"Might as well give it a shot," he murmured aloud.

Just as he did, the phantom clock struck nine. He didn't even look at his watch because it was late afternoon. He looked around but didn't see anything unusual. He went upstairs and looked into the bathroom. Nothing but his own reflection stared back at him.

He cleared his throat and spoke aloud, "I ask that you please leave this house. You're being disruptive. I promise you I will take loving care of it." He was speaking to the mysterious "she" that Diane had referenced, but he added the last part in case Richard was hanging around too.

A cold gust of air blew around him and made him shiver.

"It's time for you to leave," he said with authority. He heard a throaty, menacing laugh, but he couldn't tell if it sounded male or female. It simply sounded evil.

Then he distinctly heard someone say, "No!" Again, he couldn't tell if the voice was male or female. It just sounded angry.

He started to descend the stairs when he heard the high-pitched scream again and almost lost his footing. Frantically, he grasped the railing and recovered his balance before it was too late. The shriek had come from the basement this time.

Rhett unlocked the cellar door and listened closely. It was deathly quiet until he heard a female's whispered plea for help. He figured it was Diane again, so he was ready to dismiss it, but then a mysterious glow came into view and floated up the stairs toward him. It wasn't the same figure he'd seen before. It wasn't Diane. The spirit wore a tortured expression, and when she reached for him, he realized exactly who it was. Her hands were missing.

Just as he was about to ask her a question, a black shadow swept down over her, and her mutilated arms flew up in self-defense. She screamed in agony again, and Rhett slammed the door. He knew what he witnessed. He saw Richard Jones attack Ellie Morrison in death. He locked the door, despite knowing it wouldn't keep a ghost out, and went back to the book. Asking the ghosts to leave did no good, so he needed another course of action. As he flipped through the pages to find out what to do next, he wondered if Ellie was trapped inside the house and why. He figured she must be, because why else would she stay there with her attacker? Maybe she'd show herself again, and he could ask her why she was trapped. Then there was Richard's spirit—the thick black cloud—to deal with. Why was he staying? Was he attached to the house or Ellie? Rhett's head was still pounding, and the matters at hand weren't helping. He took two more aspirin while reading the section in the book describing what steps to take next.

The next step was to try a cleanse. He pulled the white sage out of the shopping bag, found his lighter, and lit one end. While the smoke swirled around him, he walked counterclockwise through the house and demanded again that the spirits leave. He told them to move into the light. He covered the ground floor, then upstairs, and then, with some hesitation, the basement. He didn't see or hear anything, so he thought it must have worked. However, as he was climbing the stairs, he heard furniture being moved around the living room and the shatter of his lamp. *I guess it didn't work after all.*

After putting the couch and chairs back where they belonged and cleaning up the lamp mess, he went back to the book. He read about using holy water as another method to cleanse the house. He searched the internet for the nearest Catholic church and hoped that a priest would be there and wouldn't ask too many questions.

Rhett returned home twenty-five minutes later with a cup of holy water. Luckily, no one had been around to ask questions when he filled his cup with the blessed water from the church's basin. He did take the time, though, to say a short prayer while looking up at the cross.

With his cup of sacred water, he walked back through the entire house sprinkling it all over each room, doorway, closet, and windowsill. He also remembered to sprinkle some in the attic. He prayed during the entire process, asking God to help remove the negative energy from his home. He remembered reading that he would need to get the outside of the house too, so he headed out to the yard. He did the front porch and yard before he walked a path to the back, splashing some on that porch, the siding, and the grass. When he was finished with the backyard area, he noticed Diane sitting on her grave plot.

"What are you doing?" she wanted to know.

"I'm blessing the house with holy water to rid it of the bad spirits."

Her expression was hopeful. "I wonder if that will work. Maybe this will be over for us soon."

"You have to go into the light," he told her. "We'll call upon the Archangels to show you the light, so you can leave."

He sprinkled some of the holy water onto the four graves while praying to the angels. Slowly, the other family members, including Robert and Patrick, floated out of their graves. They joined hands, watching Rhett as he continued sprinkling the blessed water and saying prayers.

At first, Rhett wondered if it was working, but then Sarah spoke.

"Goodbye," she told him with a smile and waved her small transparent hand before taking hold of Patrick's arm.

"Thank you for this," Diane said, her face contented for the first time.

"We'll never forget you or what you've done for our family," Robert added.

Patrick, too, waved while hugging Sarah.

The family clasped hands and floated up upward until Rhett could no longer see them. He simply saw a magnificent light shining down. His neighbors would undoubtedly think that it was only the sun peeking through the clouds, but he knew better.

"Now I must help Ellie," he asserted and went back inside the house as tears of happiness flowed for the released prisoners.

CHAPTER FIFTY-FIVE

Everything was quiet inside the house, so he wondered if the holy water worked. However, his question was answered with a scream followed by more maniacal laughter. This time, the noises were upstairs. He was about to go up, but then Ellie's spirit floated down the staircase.

"Please, you must help me," she pleaded again. "Stop him from tormenting me, please."

"How do I stop him?" Rhett kept his voice low, although he doubted it would do any good when it came to ghosts.

She looked over her shoulder, so he glanced in the same direction, and they both saw the dark cloud following behind her.

"Solve my murder," she cried. "You have to find the rest of me." Then she vanished into the wall, and the black haze followed after her. More ear-piercing screams erupted, and Rhett heard the chime of the clock again too.

Rhett went outside to get away from the noise and called Detective Hulsey, using the direct number on the detective's business card.

"Hulsey," the man answered.

"Hi, detective, this is Rhett Shaw. I have one more question for you. What time of death was estimated for Ellie Morrison?"

"Hmm, I'd have to look it up. Give me a second." Rhett could hear the man typing on his keyboard. "Her murder took place around 9:00 p.m. according to the M.E. May I ask why you need to know that?"

Rhett quickly responded, "I just want my book to be as accurate as possible. Thank you for your time." He hung up before the detective could ask any more questions. *So, that's why the clock chimes nine times. Now, why aren't the cleansing rituals working?*

He went back to the book for answers. He read that he may be dealing with a residual haunting where the energy is imprinted on something. Minerals, including limestone, were listed as an example. He looked down at the floor, but it was his basement that he was seeing in his mind's eye. The home was built in 1976 when limestone was used more often. The soft, porous rock explained the crumbling sections he'd seen while working on the shelving. While he hadn't seen any large sections where holes had been made, he still felt like an answer was down there.

He walked down the steps with his heart beating loudly in his ears. He turned on the light, but he'd also brought the flashlight with him just in case Richard pulled another prank. He scanned the room, paying close attention to the walls for any signs of damage. He only saw the small patches of crumbling, though, so he looked a little harder.

He walked over to the large red tool chest, which almost reached the ceiling, and cleared it out to make it light enough for him to move. He braced his shoulder against the cabinet and pushed with all his might. A loud scraping sound pierced the air as it finally gave way to his determination.

There was a large cracked area high up on the wall. Rhett grabbed the small workbench to stand on and poked his fingers into the crack until he could jimmy a large chunk of limestone out of the wall. There was a big hole behind it. He shined his flashlight into the opening and almost toppled off the bench. The light had reflected off a chunk of bone.

Cringing, he reached inside and pulled out the skeletal remains of Ellie Morrison's hands. A cloud of dust came with them and made him choke profusely. The hands were covered with cobwebs, dirt, and several diamond rings. Rhett set them on the table and shined the light back into the hole. He recovered more priceless jewelry and a thick stack of money. He was still coughing from the dust when he stood back in disbelief to examine his findings. Then he gently gathered everything together and went upstairs.

Ellie's spirit was waiting for him. Her tortured expression gave way to a peaceful smile, and she reached out to Rhett with arms that were now complete with phantom hands.

"I can't thank you enough," she sang out with a soft sigh before floating through the front door.

Rhett followed behind the spirit. He wanted to go to the police and turn the found items in. On his way out the door, he heard Richard wailing in misery. He glanced back to see the black cloud moving in his direction, so he stepped aside. The cloud didn't float up through the sky like the Jones family and Ellie had. Instead, it suddenly burst with a loud cry.

"It's Judgment Day for you, Richard," Rhett mumbled with a big smile. He turned to look at his

house before leaving, and for the first time, it
looked   content.

CHAPTER FIFTY-SIX

"**I**'m completely stunned," Detective Hulsey said when handed over the hands, stolen jewelry, and cash. His hands trembled as he tried to put on latex gloves. "Where did you say you found this?"

Rhett wore a smug smile. "I thought to look around the basement, and I found it behind the large tool chest."

"Well fuck me!" he spat. "We searched that house a couple of times, but I guess we dropped the ball when we didn't look behind the tool chest." He punched his fist on the desk, causing the other employees in the room to jump. "Was there just a hole there? Because I can't believe we missed it!"

Rhett explained the properties of limestone and described the crack he'd found in the wall. The detective palmed his forehead.

"I just can't believe it. Are you sure you weren't meant to be a cop instead of a writer?"

Rhett shrugged and laughed off the remark.

"Since you weren't wearing gloves, I'm going to need to get your fingerprints for exclusion," Detective Hulsey informed him while grabbing an ink pad and fingerprint card from his desk.

He rolled Rhett's inked fingers onto the card and then set it aside. Then he offered up a wet towelette so Rhett could clean his hands. Other detectives and patrol officers were straining to see what was going on, so Detective Hulsey stood up and made an announcement.

"This civilian just turned in critical evidence for our case against Richard Jones in the 2001 string of thefts and murders. We owe him a huge debt of gratitude."

Rhett's face turned bright red from the round of applause that followed the short speech. When it died down, he turned his focus back to the large man, who was eyeing the rings while stroking his red beard.

"I just can't fucking believe it," he said again.

"I'm happy I could help. I'll see myself out now since I know you must have paperwork to take care of for the case," he mumbled sheepishly.

"Okay, but I want to read your book, so bring me a copy when it's out," the detective called after him, and he waved in response.

GET
OUT

When he got home, it was nice and quiet. He felt alone and freed. He saw the phone number still out on his desk and decided to give Renee a call before he lost his nerve.

She answered on the second ring. "Hello?"

"Hi, Renee, this is Rhett Shaw. I hope I'm not calling at a bad time."

"No, it's good to hear from you," she cooed, and they spent the next twenty minutes talking. She invited him over for dinner that night, and without hesitation, he accepted.

"I'll see you tonight at 7:00 then," he said after she told him she had to get off the phone for an appointment. "You're never going to believe what happened to me today."

He sat back in his chair and smiled. It was difficult to imagine being in a relationship again, but he knew Laura would be happy for him because that's the kind of woman he'd married. As Renee had said over coffee, "Life has to go on."

He looked around the room; it finally felt like home. And now that he was comfortable in his home, he needed to work on his book.

He'd mentally planned out the ending during the drive home from the police station. Maybe he'd solve two cases in one day. He opened the document and began to write.

CHAPTER FIFTY-SEVEN

Jack counted his stacks of cash again and then hid them inside his mattress. He'd use the fake ID for a new bank account in the morning since he knew he was settled in for a while. His internet and cable were installed and running, so he went online and applied for a couple of credit cards under his new name, Damon Bradshaw. Eric was right about the good credit score because he was immediately approved. He chuckled at his good fortune and took a sip of his beer.

"Here's to living the dream," he toasted himself.

He plopped onto the couch and turned on his wide flat-screen TV. He flipped through the channels until he came across the local news. The reporter was covering the story about the local woman who was still missing, and Jack smiled with satisfaction.

"It was nothing," he announced.

He flipped to the history channel and saw that they were airing a documentary about Jack the Ripper. It started to give him ideas. He was considering how to up his game when a knock on the door made him jump from surprise. It was after midnight, so he couldn't imagine who it could be unless he had insomniac neighbors. *People had better not be coming here to bitch about the noise already.*

He looked out the peephole and saw two men in suits. At that late hour, it couldn't be good.

"Sorry, guys, but I'm not interested in whatever it is you're selling," he greeted them in a smug tone.

He didn't need to see their badges to know they were police officers, but they flashed them anyway.

The bigger man replied, "That's okay, sir, because we just need to talk tonight." Without being invited in, they shoved past him and entered the condo.

Jack looked out into the hallway and debated running. *They can't have anything on me. I need to relax.*

"Talk about what, officers?" he asked casually.

"We're detectives, not officers. I'm Detective Small, and he's Detective Douglas," the bigger man replied while keeping an eye fixed on him.

"All right. Well, what can I do for you, *detectives*?"

"You can tell us where you were around 10:00 p.m."

Jack tried to smile confidently, but it was forced. "I was here in my new condo. I moved in yesterday."

Detective Small bobbed his head. "Is that right? Well, it's a nice place. Now, can anyone verify your whereabouts earlier?"

Jack's palms began to sweat, and he swallowed with an audible gulp. "No. I live alone, and I haven't met the neighbors yet."

The detective smiled, but it wasn't a kind smile. It was self-righteous. "Well, here's the thing. Two eyewitnesses place you at a crime scene earlier. They saw you running to a parked car near the local furniture store. You were carrying a bank bag and wearing a ski mask."

Jack laughed nervously. "It's winter outside if you haven't noticed, but like I said, I was home, so that couldn't have been me." He stretched wide and forced a yawn. "Now, I'm ready for bed, so if you don't mind, I'd like for you to leave."

Detective Small laughed now. "Well, we're just getting started. You see, here's the thing about our witness. He's a retired police officer, and you looked suspicious, so he followed you all the way here while his wife recorded it on her phone. Then he went back and found the manager's body, so he called us."

Jack started to tremble, and his hands twitched. The gun was in his bedroom, so the only thing he could do was run. The detective read his mind.

"You could probably outrun me, but I think Ralph here could catch you, and I have two patrol cars guarding the door," Detective Small told him while pulling out a set of handcuffs. "Now, turn around and put your hands behind your back," he ordered while the other detective read Jack his Miranda rights.

Rhett leaned back in his chair and smiled. He liked wrapping up the book this way, and he was confident that Dave would like it too. He looked at the stacked journals on his desk and considered putting them back in the attic. Something, however, inspired him to keep reading.

"Hell, maybe I should write the book," he mused aloud. "Someone should tell their story."

He typed out a quick afterward for *The Edge of Reason* and sent it off to Dave with a brief note saying that now that this book was done, he had an idea for the next one that he wanted to discuss.

He opened a blank document and created his title page. He decided to call this book *Angry House,* and he dedicated it to Sarah Jones.

.